KIND ONE

Kind One

A NOVEL

LAIRD HUNT

COFFEE HOUSE PRESS
MINNEAPOLIS
2012

COPYRIGHT © 2012 by Laird Hunt
COVER AND BOOK DESIGN by Linda Koutsky

Coffee House Press books are available to the trade through our primary distributor, Consortium Book Sales & Distribution, cbsd.com or (800) 283-3572. For personal orders, catalogs, or other information, write to: info@coffeehousepress.org.

Coffee House Press is a nonprofit literary publishing house. Support from private foundations, corporate giving programs, government programs, and generous individuals helps make the publication of our books possible. We gratefully acknowledge their support in detail in the back of this book.

Good books are brewing at coffeehousepress.org

LIBRARY OF CONGRESS CIP INFORMATION
Hunt, Laird.
Kind one : (a novel) / by Laird Hunt.
p. cm.
ISBN 978-1-56689-311-4 (alk. paper)
1. Title.
PS3608.U58K56 2012
813'.6—dc23
2011046602

FIRST EDITION | FIRST PRINTING
PRINTED IN THE UNITED STATES

ACKNOWLEDGMENTS
The author would like to acknowledge the particular inspiration he derived from reading *Incidents in the Life of a Slave Girl, Written by Herself*, by Harriet A. Jacobs; *The Known World* (not limited to but in particular its eleventh page), by Edward P. Jones; *The Palm-Wine Drinkard*, by Amos Tutuola; and Marguerite Yourcenar's "Reflections on the Composition" of *Memoirs of Hadrian*. He would also like to note that the long-germinating seed for this novel of revolt was planted in 1990 in a seminar he took with Professor Richard Blackett at Indiana University, which addressed, among other slavery-related subjects, the causes and consequences of the Haitian Revolution.

Crucial support in the writing of *Kind One* was received from the division of Arts, Humanities and Social Sciences at the University of Denver.

for Lorna, sister and friend

In the evening she would tell it. In the dusk light, when the candles were lit and the fire was low, she would clear her throat. When the windows were closed and the curtains drawn and the children tucked, she would set in to speak. When we had all gathered close, when our shoulders had touched, when we had taken her hands, when we had drawn in our breath. When we had shut tight our eyes, when we had thought of our days, the years of our suffering, our joy in the sunshine, that time by the water, cool drops on our foreheads, warm bread in our mouths. When we had all been spared, when our crops had come in, when the storm had stepped past, when we had said all our prayers. When the night stretched before us, she would open her tale.

OVERTURE

(THE DEEP WELL)
1830

Sometime like apes that mow and chatter at me
And after bite me,

I SET A MARKER one hundred paces from the stream, gathered my tools, and began to dig. The earth was soft at first, and I worked fast and had dug the hole past my waist by midday when my wife called on me to wash and come into the house. We ate salt beef and cold meal cakes and drank cloudy water from the stream. After dinner I stood a time over our daughter's basket, picked her up when she started to cry, then went back out to my hole. I dug quickly until I hit a gathering of rocks that I fought for most of the afternoon. I had dug during the war and liked to dig but the rocks were wearisome, and when I came up out of the hole in the evening the pick and shovel had cut through the heavy calluses on my hands.

We ate more salt beef and more meal cakes but this time dipped them in honey. We spoke of the cloudy water, which came from the stream. It was good, but the water we would pull up from the well would be clear and always cool and delicious. Speaking of the water to come made me want to return to the hole straight after supper, but my wife told me that I must rest. So instead of returning to my picks and shovels, I went to look at the stock—three pigs, two goats, a cow—then came back to the house and played a few minutes with our daughter. She was learning to stand by pulling herself up on the chairs. I held her hands and helped her to her feet. I let her stand, teetering, by herself for a moment. She fell and rolled backwards onto her head but didn't cry. When I held out my hands she stood again. My wife came after a time and picked her up, and I took off my boots and lay down on our bed.

In the morning, while my wife and our daughter were still sleeping, I went back to the hole and picked up my shovel. I had been on a digging detail in the latter months of the second war against the English and had found it easy work. I and the men I had worked with had dug trenches and ditches and wells much like this one. I had learned from these men how to lay a filter at the bottom of the well and how to shore its walls with brick so it would hold. Some of the men had sung while they worked, and I had liked to listen to them. I was not, myself, much for singing, but my wife could sing, and after she had woken and fed the baby she came and sat near the hole and sang as she mended a pair of shoes. I liked to hear my wife sing while I worked. She would stop for a time then start up again. She liked to sing to the baby when she brought her out to sit beside her and let her play with a rattle I had made from a gourd or pull up grass in the yard. There were bees buzzing around in the airs, and I liked to think of going out to search for honey. I had watched men who kept bees, and as I dug I liked to think of building hives to have in my own yard. I had seen children help tend the hives, and I liked to think of my own daughter someday helping me to tend bees when she was older.

The walls of the well-to-be grew higher around me and I went deeper into the earth. On the evening of the third day I built a mechanism to remove the dirt and rock. I was not as good at building mechanisms as I was at digging, but the windlass I contrived was strong enough. My wife offered to haul up the dirt I put into the bucket. At first I declined. I would fill the bucket then climb out of the hole to pull it up. But the bucket was not large and pulling it up would be much less work for my wife than climbing in and out would be for me. We spoke of it over our supper of fresh milk and corn cakes fried in bacon fat. My wife said she could do it and I said I didn't like for her to have to. It was just the two of us with the baby, she said. Who else in the wide world was going to help me as the hole grew deeper? Someday we'll have all the help we'll need, I said. Someday isn't today, she said. I thought of climbing in and out of the hole each time I had a bucket to pull up. I was going to hit water soon and would be wet each time. Our daughter had begun to cry, and by the time she had quieted I had nodded my head.

The next morning my wife brought the baby's basket out into the yard, and each time I had a bucket filled she pulled it up. She sang as she did this work and I, in the shade of the hole, felt very happy. I was happy when I could hear the baby laughing or crying. Once my wife came and held the baby over the mouth of the hole so that she could see her father. The baby laughed but I could not see her face, only her curly-haired silhouette. I was standing in cool mud when my wife held our daughter over the mouth of the hole, and I shivered and after a while climbed up out of the hole and into the sun.

The next day we gathered pebbles from the streambed. I plucked them from the water and tossed them onto the bank. My wife separated them into piles by color. There were blue pebbles and pink pebbles and green pebbles and white pebbles. There were brown pebbles and yellow pebbles. The baby liked to put her hand into the piles and to put the pebbles into her mouth. She seemed to like the blue ones best. I told my wife that it wouldn't matter what their color was where they were headed, but my wife said that it would matter to her. That it mattered to her was enough for me, and I took to calling out some of the colors I pulled up from the mud. It was pleasant to be out in the sunlight, in the warmth, in the gentle stream by my wife and our child. We had our dinner by the stream. I held my feet out of the water as we ate, but my wife let hers dangle in the wet. The baby cried a little then laughed and pulled herself aloft by grabbing onto my back.

I had hoped it would be time for the pebbles but found there was still a good deal of digging to be done. Twice I came out of my hole and breathed the warm air and let the sun bake the chill out of my bones. As I sat resting I considered the mound of dirt they had made. It was taller than my head. My wife had had to walk up its side in places. I could see her footprints. I knew that if our daughter was older, she would like to play on that pile. She would finish her chores and play at climbing to the top. I was tired, but I thought of climbing to the top of the pile myself. Of jumping down to its bottom. When I was a boy, far away from this Kentucky hill country, I had once jumped off the side of my father's barn and broken my arm. None of the other boys had dared to do it. My father had whipped me until the switch broke. I did not plan to use a switch on my daughter. Even if the memory of jumping off the barn and of my father whipping me now, in the wet and dark of the hole, made me smile.

That evening I took my rifle out into the trees over the rise. The woods were quiet. I sat still for a long time. I did not know why the birds weren't singing. It was too early for them to have gone to sleep. Nothing stirred. I both liked and did not like it. We had chosen our place, far away from anyone, but not from anything. Once, as I sat, the wind shifted and I could smell the fire from our chimney. I had grown lonely in the well. I did not understand this. I had worked alone for long hours in dark places during the war and had never grown lonely. Once I had just missed being buried alive under the enemy's fortifications. I had stopped breathing when another man grabbed my boots and pulled me free. I was eager to take the pebbles down into the hole I had dug. I would do that the next day. I was glad my wife had made such pretty piles with them.

I dug again in the mud all the next long day. I had been worried about the walls of the well, but the earth was rich in clay and held firm. Roots dangled from the walls I had made, and every now and again an earthworm shivered

itself free and dropped into the water I now had to put my
shovel through. At first I tried to save these worms, as I
had when I had dug wells during the war. I picked them
up with my hands or with my shovel. I picked them up if
I could see them. Often they were just gone into the
swirling water. Soon I stopped trying to save them. I knew
I would want to be saved if I fell out of my home of earth
and into an unexpected pool of water, some wet cavern in
the dark. The light from the sunny day above came down
and lit me in my labors. The buckets I sent up were heavier than they had been before, but the windlass held and
my wife did not complain even as the dirt pile grew and
grew.

It rained the next day and the one after that. At first I
tried to continue my work, deep below the earth, but the
rain grew strong and the walls slick, and I knew I had lowered myself into a foolishness I might not emerge from. We
built a fire and sat by it. The livestock were secure and the
roof of our house did not leak. Our daughter giggled in her
basket or on our laps. My wife did her mending and we
spoke of the labors to come. I meant next to clear a fresh
field beyond the stream. I meant to erect a barn. I meant
for our stock to multiply. It rained and we spoke of days
past. My wife had lived by the sea during her youth, and
she liked to think of ways that the world around her was
like the world that lived on in her mind. She also liked the
differences between this world and that one, and I loved
her for that. When our daughter had fallen asleep and the
fire had settled into itself, we lay down together on the bed.

I waited two days after the rain had stopped and the waters had receded before returning to the bottom of the well. All that day my wife lowered buckets of colored pebbles down to me. She sent the blue ones first, then the green ones, then the white ones, then a mixture of yellow and brown. Last, she sent down the pinks. I set the pebbles down in the water by the fistful and did my best to spread them out as I thought she had imagined them. Layers of hard color the water could rise through.

That afternoon a man and a woman dressed in buckskin came out of the woods. They both wore bright feathers and pieces of colored string in their hair. They came across the field and stepped onto the yard and went to the lip of the well and looked down. Then they looked over to the house where I stood ready with my gun, but they just nodded at me and looked down the well and walked on.

As I fell asleep that night, I thought of the brick I would line the sides of my well with, but when I slept I dreamt of colored stones. Once I thought I woke during the night and called out, but I did not wake, did not call out. It seemed to me as I dug deeper into my sleep that a chink opened in the side of the house and moonlight crept in. Even though there was no moon that night and no chink for it to creep through.

I was slow to wake in the morning and slower to set to piling up bricks by the mouth of the well. I had no hod so I carried the bricks two at a time, one in each hand. I made a neat pile and checked the pulley. I considered aloud just dropping them down into the dark and following afterward, but my wife said she wouldn't like that. There was a way to dig a well, and that was the way I had been digging it. During the war I had watched men drop what they needed into wells and had no quarrel with the approach, but followed my wife's wishes. We saw that the bucket could hold three bricks at a time and she brought our daughter out and set her on the ground and told me she was ready. I was ready too and turned to climb down into the hole.

I saw the bear when I turned. It was standing beside an oak sapling, sniffing at the air. It lifted one of its paws a little as it sniffed. It looked at us, then sniffed the air in our direction. It took two steps toward us then turned and ambled slowly over to the stock pen. It set some of its weight into its haunches then swept out a forepaw and quietly stove in the fence. I could not remember afterward how it had happened, but I suddenly had the rifle in my hands. I shot the bear as it was considering the pigs. The ball did nothing and the bear continued its work. It killed two pigs, sniffed their carcasses carefully, then took the third. The other stock had pressed themselves against the fence walls, mad with fear. I was still reloading as the bear walked off into the woods with its prize. I was still reloading when my wife started to scream.

The baby had been hurt in falling, and when I carried her up out of the well she was dead. I gave her to my wife then went and leaned against the side of the house. The wood was warm from the afternoon sun. Everything below my chest was dripping. I knew our daughter was dripping too. She had struck her head in falling and had a crescent mark above her eyebrow. I turned to look and saw that my wife had not moved. I could see my daughter's leg, the soft skin above the small, wet boot. We buried her near the stream. We sat together for a long time next to the small grave. Then we went back to our house. I came back out of the house as quickly as I had entered it. I could not stand to see the baby's basket, the rattle I had made for her, the bowl I had carved. My wife asked me to come back in but I didn't. Instead I climbed down into the well. There were fresh earthworms floating in the water, but I did not save them. Instead I reached down and pulled up handfuls of pebbles and put them in my pockets. Instead I moaned and tore at my beard.

Later, although my wife asked me not to, I filled in the well. Our baby must be properly buried, I told my wife. She must be safe. And it did seem to me, during my labors and long after them, that my child was still down there, that she was crying and clenching her fists above the colored pebbles, that she was not buried safe and dry in the loamy dirt beside the stream.

Some years hence I dug another well, but I would not drink from it, nor sit at table beside any who would.

KIND ONE

(FIELD AND FLOWER)
1911 / 1850s / 1861

Sometime am I
All wound with adders who with cloven tongues
Do hiss me into madness.

1.

ONCE I LIVED IN A PLACE where demons dwelled. I was one
of them. I am old and I was young then, but truth is this
was not so long ago, time just took the shackle it had on
me and gave it a twist. I live in Indiana now, if you can
call these days I spend in this house *living*. I might as well
be hobbled. A thing that lurches across the earth. One
bright morning of the world I was in Kentucky. I remember it all. The citizens of the ring of hell I have already
planted my flag in do not forget.

Charlotte County. Ninety miles from nowhere. It was
four hundred acres, varied as to elevation, with good
drainage to a slow running creek. There was a deep well,
fine pasture for the horses. Much of the land never went
under cultivation, and there were always frogs and owls for
the night and foxes to trot bloody-jawed through the dawn.
Birds must have liked its airs, because the airs were full of
them. A firearm went off independently and we had half a
flock for supper. In season, we had fresh corn and beans
and tomatoes and squash. There was a boy who kept it all

in shape. Two more looked to the pigs. The girls cooked and kept house and kept me.

It was a pretty country. Greens were greens. There was snow for Christmas and holly bushes to make sure it looked white. Breezes and flowers for the summer. Trees in autumntime stuffed with red and yellow leaves. Bulbs to crack open the earth when it came up on spring. It has been my whole excuse for a life since I held my breath and pointed my back at that place, but my mind has never learned to hold what transpired there against it. The land is the land and the land washes itself clean. I had a father who had been through battles who told me that.

Still, even if they are all gone, even if they are all scattered or dead, I would not want to come over the rise and across the stone bridge and arrive there again. No, I would not want that.

My husband's name was Linus Lancaster, which made me Ginny Lancaster, but they do not call me that here. I live in a house on a corner of a farm that belongs to the family whose floors I scrubbed for forty years. When they come to call, which some of the younger ones still do, they stand in the yard and holler, "You in there Scary Sue?" I am. I've got a view of a barley field and a woods they haven't taken the axe to yet. I've got a little kitchen with its own pump and a place to sit on the front porch when it is too warm. I've got a shelf of books they have let me have out of the big house over the years. I'll read just about any kind of a book you could offer, but it is mostly adventures and romances that sit close to hand. Books in which they die by the cheerful dozen and the knight comes to rescue off the damsel and the good lord of hosts lets it pour down happy ever afters like there wasn't anything else in his skies. Like he didn't have any other eventualities squirreled away up there.

Linus Lancaster was my mother's second cousin. He came to us from Kentucky and grabbed me up when I was just settling into school.

"Would you do me the honor, Ginny?" he said to me.

"Yes I would," said I.

"Then come along with me and be my fair maiden," he said.

"I'll come, I will," said I.

He told my mother about his piece of paradise, said he'd struck it rich as a king in trade and now was going to let the land care for him. He had good bottom land. A

stream. A well with water so kind to the throat that it
would never let you drink anything else. Good outbuildings. Sharp ploughs and axes. China and cutlery. Larders
full. Healthy stock. People to look to it. He'd had a wife in
Louisville, but she was now his dearly departed, and each
night his soul would beg him to bring it some Christian
company. My father, the same who had been through battles, had a wooden foot and a cane to club on us with.
Linus Lancaster told my mother about Charlotte County,
but my father was there listening, quiet, the way he liked
to. With a pipe at the ready and one eye shut.

There was a good deal to say about that place in
Kentucky, and my father took it all in, every word. I mostly
looked at him and at Linus Lancaster. I liked how new
Linus Lancaster's shirt was. He had two of them in his
valise and ten more just like it, he said, in his fine home.
My mother liked to hear him talk. She got that look of hers,
like a daisy under a sweet raindrop, when he would open
his mouth and dance out at us with his tongue. My father
saw that look and he saw Linus Lancaster and he saw me,
there in my corner, mooning over it all. When it seemed
like Linus Lancaster's tongue was done with its long dancing, my father straightened up on his chair and hit a little
at the floor with his wooden foot. He looked at me, then
at Linus Lancaster, then he cleared his throat. In school, the
teacher had let me lead the lesson, my father said, opening
one eye and shutting the other. The teacher had said one
day it could be me to stand in front of the class and hold
the chalk, and what, he wondered, did Linus Lancaster

think about that. Linus Lancaster said he had heard that about me. He said he liked a woman who knew her letters. Said there was great accommodation in his heart for the delicacies of the mind.

"Do you want to go?" my father asked me later.

"Yes, I do," I said.

"I will ask you again—do you want to go down to Kentucky with this man, cousin to your mother, Linus Lancaster, to be his wife and do his bidding?"

"Yes, Father," I said.

He did not say a thing until the next day, when I was out in the goose pond with mud and wet feathers up to my elbows and all the geese honking and carrying on like I was the rapture come to smite them. My father quietly considered this carnival for a time, then he kicked at a goose come too close to his wooden foot.

"Go on then," he said.

We left a fortnight later. There wasn't much fuss to it. My mother and father, a third cousin and an uncle, a cow, the old mare, and a broken-wing chick. A turkey buzzard, looking for his lunch, haloed the house. My mother waved to her cousin with a cloth she was holding. My father pushed down his hat and held up his hand.

Everything I had fit in one half of the small trunk my father made for me after the wedding out of some wood he'd salvaged from a corn crib. As we made the drive down I would turn often and look at my trunk bouncing there in the back of Linus Lancaster's wagon and wish that I could take off my new traveling hat with its pink ribbon, open the trunk, wrap my arms around myself, and curl up inside. If I had, maybe my body would have kept some of that which wasn't books, sturdy notions, or linens from breaking into the little bits of nothing I found after I pulled up the nails when we arrived.

Linus Lancaster had his girls get me settled. His house wasn't what he had told my mother about. There weren't any columns or gables or fifty-foot porch to it. It was just a cabin with a long corridor and some extra rooms tacked on. But they kept it well. You could make a breeze run in through the windows and down the hall, and the country when I first came to it was fragrant. That was the thing I liked best in those first days. I liked to stand at a window and bite off pieces of that breeze. That was a breeze to chew on and think about and swallow. Never mind that winter hadn't come yet to freeze it all until your teeth would snap straight off in your mouth if you smiled. Never mind that there would be more than breezes to trot along that corridor in the jolly days to come.

"Welcome," those girls said, then each tried their hand at a curtsy. They were just little bitty things then. Ten and twelve. I was fourteen.

In the big house that sits one Christian mile due east of this little house and this scrawly stretch of barley that the rabbits like to visit, there is the big shelf of books that is the mother to the little shelf I have here. It isn't just my happy books on that big shelf. It is other things. It is the shallow and the deep parts of the pocket both. After I had gotten myself up here and had started in to scrubbing floors, on that shelf I searched every day for the word to say what it was that befell us in that house in Kentucky. I looked in every book for that word, but I did not see it. It wasn't until a Sunday at the church that I learned what that word was and saw that I had looked at it many times in those books and heard it said every day.

It was a kind of spring morning with a kind of warm sun and we had all spilled ourselves out of the church, and I was waiting for them to finish their quiet talking so we could get home and look to dinner when Mr. Lucious Wilson, my employer and the owner of this little house and this barley field and all that surrounds it and the whole wide world for all I care, called over to me, "Come on out of that shadow and into this sunshine."

So I thought, yes, *shadow* is the word and I have seen it and I have heard it before and thought it before but now I know it. It has been said.

Shadow.

Which is where I've been and where I am and where I'm wending my sorry way. So if I say I can look now at my earliest days in that place in Kentucky at the home of my husband Linus Lancaster and see the light of a pretty, unhurt place shining on us all, you can know and I can say that this is just tricks from a mind that wants what was to be otherwise but can't change it.

If I say that in my early days there was a meadow where I would walk with the girls, Cleome and Zinnia, to look out for daisies, and where we would sit together of a morning and make chains that could have stretched all the way to Louisville, you would be right to look me square in my shadowy eye and say you don't believe me. If I tell you that in those days I would go to look at the colts when they were dripping fresh, with Cleome and Zinnia to my sides or me to theirs, and that we would pick big tomatoes for the table out of little Alcofibras's gardens and play in the yard at weighing them on the market scales or go together to the woods to look for mushrooms or lie as flat as you like on our backs by the creek or hold hands and skip like faeries and flap our arms together like blue jays or hold our faces up to the falling snow like three fingers of the same fork, you will say, and I will nod, that it cannot have been.

There is a shadow covers it all now.

There was already shadow deep enough to drown in back then.

Drown me and those girls. Drown little Alcofibras. Drown those daisies. That meadow. Those tomatoes. That sun.

Cleome and Zinnia helped me get settled at the home of Linus Lancaster, and they helped me when he commenced to have me into his bedroom.

They helped me, but I never helped them.

That is not true. That is not the truth's only portion, not the whole of it. I helped them in those years that came by helping them in other ways. I helped them when they had the fever headache or when they had the ague or when they had the festery eye. I helped them when the tobacco grew so thick they cried to contemplate the day that had to be spent in it, or when there were too many hides to tan, or too much corn to put up, or a biting goat that needed chasing, or a pig that was too mean.

Zinnia hated icicles, was afraid they would fall on her hat and pierce through her head, so when they got too big and it was her had been set to knocking them off the eaves, and Cleome and the others were at some other work, it was me went around whacking at them with the broom. I like the sound of an icicle hitting snow. The kind of long cave it will make. How it will keep a week without melting when it lies inside that softer cold.

I helped them with their first girl sicknesses, told them, as my mother had told me, what it was they had to do. They took my hand and thanked me for that. Each one of them in her turn. I think Zinnia's eye might have sprung a tear. Little bitty thing like a ball of dew. I helped them with that and I helped them sweep and I helped them pluck and I helped them darn and I helped them sew.

I helped them in those ways and in others, and once one rosy summer day when Linus Lancaster was looking for her with a switch in his hand, I didn't tell him I'd seen Cleome drop the bucket into the well and dangle herself down its rope.

"What did you do?" I said, after Linus Lancaster had got tired of yelling and chasing and dropped his switch and gone off to swear and smoke in the woods. Cleome was deep down in the well, her feet almost tickling the water.

"I spilled coffee on his shoe, then I made him trip when I was cleaning it up," she said.

"Sounds like maybe you deserved some switching," I said. I laughed when I said this and added on for merry measure that I thought a switch or two seemed a small thing to make her creep all the way down a well. She did not laugh though, just looked up at me. There was a cold coming up with her eyeballs out of the dark. Cold made me think of one of those icicle caves. After a while, so you can see how truth has its portions, meager may they be, I steadied the rope and helped her climb back up.

I told it earlier that my teacher in Indiana at the little brick school I used to go to before I joined Linus Lancaster in his paradise had let me lead the lesson. She had let me lead the lesson and had invited my parents in to hear it, and my father came and sat in the back and heard the teacher tell the class that at least she had one pupil that had a head and not a stuffed feed sack to do her thinking with. I had written down a story about a princess who came by luck and cunning and other such foolery to be queen of the clouds, and the teacher had me read that after I had led them all through letters and numbers and the naming of the countries of the world. I had written down that story while the others of them had frolicked to no clear purpose, the teacher said. I had sat on my bench and composed that story, and now we had heard it and were the better, every last one.

When we got back home my mother asked my father, "How was the show?"

"That's about what it was," my father said. He put his hand a minute on my arm when he said this. Then he let it go.

Often was the time in those early days in Kentucky that I thought about that story I had written and about that day in the school. I told Cleome and Zinnia about it and they made me tell it again and again for the several days after.

"I'd like to live up on one of those clouds," Cleome said.

"And drink up that lemonade," said Zinnia.

"We could all live up there together," I said.

They had me tell it to Alcofibras, but he just shook his head and said clouds were cold places to live.

I also told my husband, Linus Lancaster, who appreciated the delicacies of the mind even as he kept his hand always near a switch, as he was at his supper. He heard it and looked at me twice or thrice, then got up, walked to my trunk, fished the four or five books I had brought up out of it, and heaved them over into the stove.

"No more clouds now, Ginny," he said. Then he called for his bath, and I knew it was time for me to go and wait for him in the bedroom. When he came into the bedroom, fresh from his bath, my husband made himself ready before me. He liked to stand, at the ready, in his nothings. And he did this for a time that night. Then he drew the covers back and lay down.

"We have the Bible for stories, Mrs. Lancaster," he said to me after. "Look to those good words and to those good words alone now. There wasn't any book but the good one for my dearly departed, and there won't be any other for you."

But there was no book good or otherwise in that cabin with its long corridor. I looked all the next day for it. The girls said they had never seen any good book in Linus Lancaster's house and wouldn't speak a peep to whether or not his dearly departed had had one. When I inquired to him about it he said it was here somewhere, he'd had it out recently, and that if I was too rearward to find it that was none of his affair. Then he had me back into his bed.

When Linus Lancaster was in trade in Louisville and still sharing his table with his dearly departed, he made the money he did make in the barter of livestock, and that was when he started dreaming about his place in paradise that would take care of him like the ancient lands took care of the Israelites. He told me this the first time in his bed with his arms on my shoulders and his face over mine. He also told me that it was after he had started to conjuring this way that he had fallen asleep one night and seen a countryside covered in pigs. The land, he told me, was green and the pigs roamed the land and there in the middle of it stood the shining house he would tell his second cousin, my mother, about as my father listened.

When I first arrived at his home he had not yet made good on his dream. There were chickens and cows and horses but no pigs. Then one afternoon he had a load of lumber and nails in, and the next morning he set Ulysses and Horace to building pens and sheds. One week later they all came, weeping and grunting like babies lost from heaven. The man who had driven them to us stayed for a week to show Linus Lancaster how it was done. They would rise early and go out to the pens and smoke and kick or coo at the pigs. The man ate at our table and winked at me, and one night after Linus Lancaster had retired with a poor tooth took Cleome by the waist and dandled her on his knee and would have done more than dandle, but he had drunk all we had and fell over onto the floor. The next day the man left the pigs he had brought to us behind and headed back down the road with his switch.

On taking his leave he told Linus Lancaster that pigs never brought anything but peace to a man, and Linus Lancaster, who that very afternoon would have Ulysses yank that tooth from his mouth with a pair of tongs, said, "We'll see."

We did. You could see those pigs turning the greensward to filthy froth from the room where Linus Lancaster kept his bed. He liked to sing a little after he'd been in at me. He didn't sing loud enough but what you could still hear those pigs snuffling and snoring in their pens. In the morning, maybe after he'd been at me again, he liked to go out and stand at the fences and sing and consider them.

They don't all call me Scary here. That's just the younger ones. The name I gave when I came up out of Kentucky and floated my sorry way north was just Sue. I gave them that name, which had been the name of that schoolteacher who had let me lead the lesson, because it was the first thing that came into my head when they asked me what I was called. I had not made any plan. I had not thought it through. My own old name had not come to me when I was asked, and after a minute the other one had. So it was Sue this and Sue that for my first years here, and then one of the little ones had come up on me when I was on my knees scrubbing and had my skirts lifted up over my ankles and saw the dark red ring just above my ankle bone. She saw it and said, "What is that?"

"That is what you call a scar," I said.

"It looks all scarry," she said.

"That's just right, it is all scarry," I said.

And I thought we had left it there. Only the next time I saw her she called me Scarry Sue, and some other of my employer Lucious Wilson's children heard it and thought his sister had said Scary or liked it better that way, and then they were all calling me that.

"Tell us a story, Scary Sue," they would say. "Scary Sue, fetch us some of that popcorn. Scary Sue, give us our bath."

Lucious Wilson would have put a stop to it, but after the second or third time I heard him scolding I told him it didn't matter and that I wasn't hurt by it. He ought to let them call me what they wanted—they didn't mean any harm. I told him I knew something about what harm was, and it didn't have anything to do with his children and some name.

He didn't argue. He knew about the scar on my ankle and he knew that whenever it started to settle I would give it a few fresh licks. He had walked in on me going after it one sunny Saturday not long after I had arrived. Had stood watching me let it bleed into my sock. Stain the bedsheets. Feed the floors. Drip through the tunnels. Head to the underparts of Kentucky. Talk to the worms.

"What are you doing, Sue?" he had asked.

"Traveling, Mr. Lucious Wilson," I had answered.

"All right," he had said.

Scary wasn't wrong.

2.

IT WAS OF A MORNING that Linus Lancaster was singing and conducting his considerations out by the pigpens in nothing but his work britches that my mother and my father came rolling over the stone bridge in the old cart they'd driven down the long road from Indiana. They rolled slow down the lane and took the look of the place and then a look at Linus Lancaster in his work britches standing bare foot beside the pens. I was in the kitchen with the girls and came out and watched Linus Lancaster pull his hands out of his pockets and approach the cart and call out a greeting and help my mother, his second cousin, down. You would have thought by the way he offered his bare arm to my mother and the way she took it that he was leading her to the big house he'd bragged about to her. My father came crippling on along behind them, and you didn't have to squint to see what he thought of where the road and river crossing down from Indiana had taken him.

They had come for a look-see and a visit with their son-in-law and his wife, my mother said when Linus

Lancaster had conducted them through the door and sequestered them at the table in the kitchen.

"You have apprehended me in my morning wear," Linus Lancaster said.

He had sat down with them at the table in his bare feet and britches. He was nothing but muscle from one long end of him to the other. You could see like he was shouting it that my father would have wanted for nothing better than to pull off his wooden foot and take a turn at Linus Lancaster with it. I could see his mind had already hefted it over his head and brought it down. Instead he said, "We rode that cart five days to see your mansion and your fair fields, Son-in-law."

"The mansion," said Linus Lancaster, lighting up his pipe, "lacks nothing but the building. And as for my fields, they are fair. I will show them to you. They are the fairest in all of Charlotte County."

My father said nothing to this but pulled out his own pipe and reached into the bag of tobacco Linus Lancaster held out to him. For her part, my mother saw Horace and Ulysses tending to the horses and Alcofibras walking by with a well bucket and Zinnia working at the stove and Linus Lancaster with all his muscles and said, "You have a fine number of help. I expect it is just the number you will need for your new home when it is built."

They stayed with us for a week. My mother fussed alongside me at whatever I was doing and my father clucked his tongue, shook his head at the pigs, and took long cripple walks in the woods. When I was a girl I had liked to play at following behind my father, ghosting along in his tracks as he went his ways, and I took a turn at it on the second day of that visit. My father went his crippling path over the bridge and into the woods, and when he had got past the first hickories I stepped out after him. I'd been helping hang linens, but I just left the girls to their work and went walking. It wasn't any trick to follow. My father's wooden foot was narrow at the bottom, and when there was any wet to the ground it would sink on in and pull out clumps. I followed the clumps and divots and by and by, even though he'd had a start on me, I caught my father up. When I was little I had liked to holler out at him when I got close, and he had liked to pretend he didn't know I'd been behind him, even though he had known it all along. When I saw my father on up a little ways, I thought, "And now I will holler and now he will turn and act like I've scared him, and now I will be back home in the goose pond again."

I opened my mouth and got fixed to holler, "Hey, Papa," even though I didn't know if that was what I still ought to call him, and then I saw that my father was not alone. That he was standing in the shade of a hickory with Alcofibras. That he was talking to him and nodding his head, and Alcofibras was talking back to him and nodding his own. They talked, and that holler I had planned fell out of my mouth and died its death on the dirt floor, and I turned around as quiet as I could go, but when I looked over my shoulder they were both of them looking the whites of their eyes at me. I don't know why, but when I saw that they had seen me I gave out a kind of squawk and took it in my head to run. I ran so hard and so fast that I lost my breath and got turned around and might have spent the night in the wood except that after a time here came Alcofibras. He didn't say a word and didn't stop, just looped a loop at the top of his walk and, when he saw that I was going to follow him and not run off again, went back the way he had come.

I am old like I said and can barely bend over to see my boot, but here is a dream in which I run: Linus Lancaster is out by his pigs and Lucious Wilson is standing next to him. They are talking and they turn and look at me. I can't move and they turn away and I can move again. Then I run. I run out the front door of this house here in Indiana but out into the yard of that other in Kentucky. I run up the road to the stone bridge there, then I am in the barley field here. I stumble and fall by the oak tree there. Linus Lancaster is leaning against the tree. He is shrugging his shoulders and easing some itch he has. I raise myself up and he nods and I am on the road that leads to Lucious Wilson's house. I run as fast as I can up that road and see that I am in Linus Lancaster's field. I run past his horses and through his grasses and his daisies and find I am in Lucious Wilson's barn. His barn has grown bigger than it ought to be and I run across it, past its pens and the hooks hanging sharp on its walls, and see that I am in Linus Lancaster's shed. My ankle hurts but I run and find myself in Lucious Wilson's barn. I run and find myself back in Linus Lancaster's shed. The shed is big and I run across it. Then the shed fills with pigs and I have to run across their backs. They are wet from the slops they have been fighting over. I slip to the floor and Lucious Wilson throws me an axe to cut my way through. I catch it and see Linus Lancaster standing with his back to me and I swing. I swing and hit pig and the earth opens up and I drop and fall and am far below its surface. There is a way forward. Something is behind me but it is not a pig. It is not Linus

Lancaster either. "Scary Sue, Scary Sue," calls a voice I do not recognize. In this running dream I cannot turn my head.

On the fourth day of my parent's Kentucky visit, Linus Lancaster got us all into his wagon and we went off to the fair. My father did not want to go to any fair, but Linus Lancaster encouraged him and showed him the big bag of tobacco he had at the ready, and in the end he came along. You had to ride a whole half a day and then some to get to that little cornbread crumb of a settlement. It was called Albatross. They were having their fair at the far side of it. They had it in a field that was next to nothing but a barn and a smoky-colored hill. When Horace had let us down, he took the wagon over and set with the other help at the base of the smoky-colored hill. The help weren't let to come into the rows of tents where they had candy in buckets and colored strings hanging and men calling out to come in and see their show. My father took his look around and said he would just as soon clump up the hill and sit with Horace, but Linus Lancaster said that wasn't the way of it here.

"The way of it here," my father said as he clumped alongside me. "I've been to a kind number of places they call 'here' the way your husband, Linus Lancaster, does, and I know something about the ways of it too."

My mother had Linus Lancaster's arm. She had had it for most of their visit. She came about as high up on Linus Lancaster as I did. We followed them into a show about a fish man they'd had up from the bottom of a pond in China. The fish man didn't have hands, he had flippers. He was blind on the top of it and had been born without a tongue. They kept him in a barrel filled with water. The water in the barrel looked black. It looked cold. My mother said, "Oh my," and we walked back out.

At one end of the fair they had a stage set up, but there wasn't anything on it. Linus Lancaster asked a man what they had planned for the stage, but the man said that there wouldn't be anything on that stage until the next day. Linus Lancaster stood for a long time looking at that stage. I thought about him looking at his pigs and reckoned he might step up and start singing. My mother asked him what he had in mind as he stood there, but he just laughed and galantried himself back on over to her and we all walked off. Every now and then as he was clumping next to me, my father would look up at the smoky hill then look over at Linus Lancaster and cluck his tongue. I said we ought to buy a sack of candy to take back to the girls, but Linus Lancaster opined to us all he'd as soon feed up some of the fine apples they had on sale to his pigs.

"A pig is good people," he said.

"Now I've heard every last thing there is to hear," my father said.

"I doubt that."

"Then tell me some more."

But Linus Lancaster didn't say another word.

Late that night when we got back in the girls were waiting with a hot supper for us. Cleome dished it up and Zinnia set it down and filled the cups and kept them filled. After Linus Lancaster was in his drink and draping his long self over the table end, my father took a piece of candy out of each of his pockets and gave it to the girls. Then he

looked at Linus Lancaster asleep there in his drink and
laughed. He laughed so long and hard that after a while it
seemed like that laugh had left away from him and had
hitched up its skirts and was dancing with hard boots on
the table in front of us. That laugh danced so hard across
the table I was afraid the cups would fall over onto the
floor and break.

"Shush now, Papa," I said.

He was old too early and crippled, but that laugh was
something. Cleome and Zinnia both watched that laugh
dance and both took their candies out of their aprons and
slowly commenced consuming them. I expect they didn't
even know they'd done it until their mouths woke up into
all of that flavor and reached down their throats and
pinched.

The next day Linus Lancaster took us on a tour of the
house that wasn't but that he said would soon someday be.
We walked in its corridors and took the airs of its rooms.
We climbed its stairs and stood in the Charlotte County
sunshine on its balconies and looked out into the distances
of Linus Lancaster's fields. Come suppertime Linus
Lancaster had Ulysses fetch up a table, and we broke our
pork and corn pone in the middle of the future banquet
room. My father went along on this tour and snorted not a
whit when my mother, dangling like ivy off Linus
Lancaster's arm, would marvel at the line of a wall that
wasn't any more than some milkweed floating through a
sunbeam or nod at the clean crack of the glistening hard-
wood floors we were none of us walking on. He even, at

one point, when we were touring the airy attics, commented on the quality of the underroof and the clean lines of the ceiling beams.

It wasn't until Linus Lancaster was again asleep at the end of his own table, a line of hard drink and slobber curling off his lip, that my father opened his mouth and let the laugh back out again. This time it didn't content itself with dancing on the table but went off dancing through the house meant to be towering everywhere around us. It danced up the stairs and out the windows and down the halls and across the rooms. Then it led us away from that table set in the middle of the dirt yard, Horace and Ulysses toting Linus Lancaster, my mother fussing next to them, back to the cabin where we all lay ourselves down.

"I heard you laughing, both times," Linus Lancaster said to my father the next day as they sat together in the yard smoking their pipes.

"I know you did," my father said.

"If you were any other than my father-in-law I would whip you for it."

"I expect you would try."

"Old cripple like yourself."

"Like I said it, you would try."

"I saw you handing out candy too like this was your own house."

"It was either that or feed it to your pigs. And how would you have felt about that?"

"Now, the both of you two," my mother said.

"It's all right," said Linus Lancaster.

"Yes it is," my father said.

There wasn't anything much more to that visit from my mother and my father. On the morning they were getting settled out to leave, I told them I was sorry to watch them go and hoped my husband and I could repay the fine courtesy they had paid us one of these times. My father was over next to me when I said this, and he turned and said that he was not sorry. That all he could see in this place with its fine fields and mansions and pigs was dark, and that more dark was coming. I ought never to have left them, and he had his own fault in that, but now that I had I could never come home. There was things in this world and in the other that got started and couldn't get stopped.

"Let me look at you now, Daughter," he said.

He put his hands on my shoulders and looked at me. He leaned his head close to mine. I leaned my own closer to his.

"Follow us," he said. He whispered it.

I leaned closer.

"Follow us away on out of here, Daughter. I will slow the wagon. Follow us like you did when you tracked me through the wood."

My father had my own green eyes and I could see mine in his, and we leaned there together as my mother and Linus Lancaster stood off at some distance and looked on. "Hey, Papa," I thought. I could hear myself holler it. But I heard it as if I was standing down at the bottom of a hole or somewhere under the waters, and hadn't I just those days before stood there and watched my holler from the past die its death on the forest floor?

"I am married now, Father," I said.

"And living in that fine house," he said.

I did not answer this. We stood on there in the morning light a minute, then he turned.

"All right, I've had my look," he said, then clumped up into the cart, and my husband, Linus Lancaster, handed up my mother and nodded at my father, and they clicked the horses and went off back over the stone bridge. I never saw one nor the other of them again.

There is a boy here works for Mr. Lucious Wilson who can sing. They say he came out singing and never quit. He has sung at the county fair and won himself an invitation to sing at the statehouse. I have heard him at the church, which is one of the places I do still go. They like to all go quiet now and again so he can have the show. It is a pretty kind of singing and a pleasant kind of voice. But when I lie down at night and think of that singing and the kind of singing Linus Lancaster could do at that place in Kentucky I know that the boy they stop the piano at church for here doesn't have half the gift. Linus Lancaster could sing the skin off of one back and onto another. He told it once when a tinker was visiting and they were at the bottle that in Louisville he spent his share of time on the stage making speeches and singing, and that there were fine ladies of the neighborhood in attendance who had cried when he had done so. I did not cry when I listened to Linus Lancaster sing. But I listened and knew I was hearing something.

There were times after supper when Linus Lancaster would push back from the table and make a sound in his throat and give a curl to his lip, and we all knew it was time for a song. Horace and Ulysses could strum and thump when they were on their own time, and Cleome liked to clap and Zinnia to sing in a slow, private way, but it was all quiet when Linus Lancaster got the mood on him to sing after his supper. No one in that house made a sound when Linus Lancaster pushed his chair back and sucked in his air and blew that trumpet out of his throat. There were no uh-huhs or mmm-hmms, and if there was a drop of sweat tickling some lip or a fly biting at some neck the song was over before any of us moved.

Someone once told me when I was still living in my father's house that I had a handsome voice and ought to shepherd it and not keep it to myself. After that I sang a little louder at our church and took a turn at a solo at my school. One night my first winter in Kentucky I thought to share that solo with my husband when that singing mood came upon him after his supper. He had not favored my story, but I thought he might favor my song. I sang and reckoned it was fair crooning, but Linus Lancaster's fist came out so fast I thought an angel of the Lord had flown down off his shoulder to bestow its wroth. Even after Cleome, who was standing in attendance, had helped me back to my bench and my husband had wiped his hand and recommenced singing I thought this. I thought it then and now here it still sits. Funny how you can once think a thing then never see the tail of it.

My father liked to say God lived in the lightning and look out below. He told it that in the battles he fought when there was lead or arrows in the air the boys used to holler, "He's a-comin'!" They get roused up when the fellow at church here sings "Mine Eyes Have Seen the Glory." But I keep quiet when he's at it. There's different kinds of glory. There's all kinds. I have seen some.

3.

MR. LUCIOUS WILSON, my employer, has pigs. He's got his
pens and fences and keeps them nice, and people come
from around to look at them. If I understand it correctly,
in recent times he's had pigs that have earned prizes. For
what I didn't catch, but there were ribbons involved, and
Lucious Wilson's man responsible got a cash bonus and
went out cavorting and kissed a girl and spent the night in
a ditch. They found his horse five miles away eating at a
patch of lawn grass. On account of some pigs.

Time and again when I was still working in Lucious
Wilson's big house I would hear it when they would stick
one. Now that is a sound can make me cringe. I understand
that there are things that live and things that get killed.
That's God's plan, and we are all just meat for his platter,
well and good. When they slaughtered beef and the beef
knew it was coming there was a bellowing in the yard to
beat the basket, but they could have killed beef from there
until Sunday and I would have kept scrubbing and dusting
and setting out the silver or whatever else my employer

Lucious Wilson requested that I accomplish. But let that weather get cold and let them start in on one pig and then another and then a third and all of them doing their dying at once, and I would commence to pick at my ankle and decompose in my shoes.

Pigs are smart, and there is a sound that pigs being killed emit and I've got the evil rhyme to that particular complaint in my head. Now I live in this little house and do not go to the big house any longer and do not hear it when they put the chisel to their pigs, or smell it when they cut out the chitterlings and scrub the insides, or feel it when they push the pork pieces into the salt. There's some will do backflips about a bacon breakfast, but I've still got teeth enough to get that product stuck between. I've still got a tongue to taste the pork blood and eyes to see the red come bubbling up out of the fresh meat when it's pressed down with a finger or a fork. Lucious Wilson is as close as you can come to a saint on this earth, but I could do without his pigs and the place they give him in my running dream.

At Linus Lancaster's home in Charlotte County, Kentucky, we ate pork morning, noon, and night. We ate it fresh, we ate it cured, we ate the cracklings, we ate the salty dribblings over our bread. We sat in the yard with pork in our hands, and we pulled it out of our pockets and ate it by the creek. What we didn't eat we wore. Horace had a hand for turning leather. One Christmas he made me the prettiest pair of boots. You could walk all day in the puddles in those boots and not get wet. Linus Lancaster got a sheath for his knife and Cleome a pair of shoes. Horace had been in a squabble with Zinnia about something or the other, and all she got was a hat chucked out of the scraps. She wouldn't wear it until Linus Lancaster made her.

The hat was a kind of droopy thing. It didn't look an inch like my boots or Linus Lancaster's sheath or Cleome's shoes. Zinnia said she didn't want to wear those old pork flaps and spit when she said it but Linus Lancaster put her in the shed for three days and three nights, and when she came out she walked straight over to Linus Lancaster and took it from him and put it on. There were rats in the shed. There was a chain at the back and that's where Zinnia was. It was a heavy chain. It had thirty-seven and a half heavy links. Cleome cried when Zinnia was in the shed, until my husband hit her with his riding crop and said he would build another shed next to the one Zinnia was in and fill it to the top with rats and throw her into it and then build another one even bigger and with even more rats and toss her into that one next, and then he would take the keys to her shackles and drop them down the well and then she could cry all she liked.

"Down the well, you hear me?" he said.

Cleome came to me after this fine speech as I stood in my pretty boots and asked me would I tell Linus Lancaster to let her sister out. Horace came with her and said he had been at fault for making her that ugly hat. It had been a mean trick, and he was sorry. We could all of us hear Zinnia in the shed. She sang in that private way as she sat in there. Some of them were the songs Linus Lancaster liked to sing, only when she sang them it was like old earth sprinkling through the air.

"She's just in there, she's not far off, wait a spell," I told them.

Linus Lancaster liked us all to take a turn at the killing. He said if we were all going to eat pig and wear pig finery then we all ought to kill it. Those of us who ate the most ought to kill the most. That was me and it was Linus Lancaster. The years went by and we ate and ate, and so we killed and killed. In the early times we killed with the chisel or the axe when they weren't looking and later with Linus Lancaster's rifle. The rifle wasn't much, and you had to be better at it than I was to do much more than set a pig off its feed. So you had to reload, take aim, and fire again. Linus Lancaster liked to have some sport with it, and more than once would climb up on a tree or a roof with his rifle and take his several shots at them.

The pigs would emit a sound when we were robbing the life out of them, and that sound is the one that is still sitting here in my head. A pig is a sensible beast. It knows what you are doing to it and it knows the why. A pig gets a look. It has seen what has been done to its fellows. It has seen them hanging up to drain in the sun. It has eaten what's left of its brothers in its slops. A pig will tell you plain that you have come to it on hell's orders and that hell is where you will return and that you with your pockets full of dried pig and your stomach full of cracklings will be comfortable there.

"I'm asking you, please, Miss Ginny," said Cleome.

"Please, Miss Ginny," said Horace.

"She's practically right out here with us, you can hear her can't you?" I said.

I met a man in Indianapolis once who told it that when you had a hard thing in your head you had to scratch at it here and scratch at it there then dig your fingers into it and yank. This hard thing in my head is also in my arms and elbows and fingertips and ankles, and how do you get that kind of a thing out? There were vegetables in Alcofibras's garden at Linus Lancaster's place in Kentucky that took a kind of nursing to get out of the ground. Carrots that had more than one root. Turnips grown too big to just tug. There wasn't anything that Alcofibras couldn't get out of the ground whole. He had a way. It was almost like he was requesting that the foot-long sweet potato come out and take the air and kindly not break as it was doing so. I expect that if he had set down cross-legged and commenced to blow a tune on a flute the whole garden would have come up and danced for him. Maybe I ought to find a way to set down next to myself and blow on a flute. Or maybe it's just yanking that's the way to get it done.

I was twenty and Cleome and Zinnia were sixteen and eighteen when Linus Lancaster commenced to paying them visits. He had been trying on me for six years and one night he pushed me out of his bed and onto the floor and told me to go and sleep in my room and one of those next nights he went over and saw Zinnia, and because Cleome and Zinnia shared one room, when he was done visiting Zinnia he sang lying there between them awhile then rolled up over onto Cleome. I know this because the real house Linus Lancaster had on his piece of heaven in Kentucky was about the size of a thimble and had walls no thicker than wax paper, and the room he had those two girls in was no more than a good spit away from my own. I didn't hear a sound in that room except for Linus Lancaster. I expect that's what they had been hearing those years he had more or less nightly and morningly been trying in on me. Some fast breathing and snuffling then those grunts he liked.

During all those years of nights and mornings while he liked to go in after me I would pass the time while he was breathing and snuffling and grunting in imagining I was elsewhere someplace. Maybe I was home at my father's house outside Lawrenceburg and was just sitting somewhere quiet and practicing my lessons or writing my story about the clouds and getting fixed to read it to the school. There was a crabapple tree I had liked to sit under in the heat and think about my lessons when I had completed my chores. Some of the books Linus Lancaster had burned up for me in his stove had been read under that tree. I had practiced my singing there. Hymns and hot glories and such. There was also my bed in the corner of the little room where I had always slept just exactly like a stone. Other times I thought about my first months in Kentucky and the breezes and sitting in the fields with Cleome and Zinnia, and that is exactly the place my mind went when I was lying there alone in my room after Linus Lancaster had kicked me, his lawful wife, out of his nightly concerns and walked down the hall to their room that first time to pay a visit.

The three of us would sit in a field and play at making daisy chains and daisy crowns, and one morning, because

Zinnia had made the prettiest crown I ran back to my chest
in the house and pulled out a spool of heavy purple thread
I'd had from my mother and brought it to Zinnia for a
prize. I put it in her hand and had to close her fingers over
it because she didn't believe it was hers to keep. She had
big hands even then, and when I closed her fingers over the
spool it disappeared and all you could see was a whisker
of purple thread spilling out over the crook of her thumb.
Linus Lancaster paid his visit, and I lay there alone and so
peaceful it hurts my head bones to remember it even now
and thought about Zinnia's big hand, which had grown
ever more over the years, and the piece of purple thread,
frayed at the end, fretting a little in whatever fine breeze
there was. She thanked me until I thought I would fall over
with it then asked if I minded whether she shared some of
it with Cleome. I told her it was hers, and if it was hers
she could do with it what she liked, but that this was a day
for prizes all around. I said this and fetched another spool,
this one red. Cleome clapped when I gave it to her and
they took pieces of their thread and wove them into the
daisies and we all three stood up with crowns on our heads
and took hands and turned a circle around and around.

It was Cleome and Zinnia had taught me that trick
about thinking yourself into someplace else. They taught
me that when they were ten and twelve and I was fourteen
and they came up on me crying one skylark afternoon in
the bloom of my youth there in that place in Kentucky. I
told them that Linus Lancaster had started his husband
ways and that I was ready to die if he kept up with them.

They each one of them put their hand on my arm and didn't say a word then let their hands drop and looked at me then at each other, and Cleome said Zinnia had told her in the old days at Linus Lancaster's home in Louisville, when she had spilled a bucket of peas and taken her long turn in the dark and stink of the coal cellar where you couldn't even stand up and didn't want to sit down, that she had to put her mind someplace else.

"What place?" I said.

"Any place ain't that place," Zinnia said.

"Pretty place," Cleome said.

"Place maybe you been dancing."

"Place like this."

So as I lay there twisting old dead daisies and not moving and not lifting a finger and not doing a thing while Linus Lancaster was in there at them, I knew they weren't in there with him beyond the flesh God had seen fit to drape them in, and that instead they were out twisting their own daisies and turning circles in the fields with me.

Yes, that first night I thought that.

It wasn't long after those visits started that Linus Lancaster turned his pigs free. He'd had them in their pens and had Horace and Ulysses build them more pens and the herd had flourished, and we had eaten of it until there was pig dripping out of our pores, and there had been the good Lord's years of that. Then one afternoon he walked out and opened the gates and forbade anyone from closing them up again or slopping the pigs to tempt them to stay, and from that day on we had pigs everywhere.

"I had to be square with my dream," Linus Lancaster told me after he had done it. "Having the pigs was the smaller portion of it. I needed to see them let loose and people the earth."

"They are your pigs and this is your land and everything in it is yours, Husband," I said.

Linus Lancaster turned to me and smiled when I had made this remark. This was at a supper. There was stuck pig spread before us. Pig milk and molasses in our cups. There wasn't a bit that was lacking. Since he'd been in at them he'd had Cleome and Zinnia sit down to table with us.

"What you say is true, Wife," he said. He had his bottle beside him. The bottle was filled with what Ulysses made out of a still he kept behind the barn. You could smell the concoction through the bottle glass, and once I saw a sparrow take two wet pecks of it and fall over dead.

"We are a family," Linus Lancaster said. "We four of us right here and the boys. I am the head of the family, and that is right and proper, but you, Wife, are its mother. The

Lord in his mansion above has decreed it that you will not carry for him, not for him nor for me. He has said it that your duty is otherwise. You, Wife, the Lord has written in his tablet, are mother to these girls. You are mother to us all."

Linus Lancaster took a drink out of his bottle and belched his benediction out at us. Not a one of us said a word. Linus Lancaster had almost put me through the door I was leaning against the day before when I had not greeted him with what he had called the due respect. Cleome and Zinnia had to my knowledge not spoken above a whisper since Linus Lancaster's visits had commenced, and if they said anything at that moment it was thrown out on their breath to the untouched plates of pork and black-eyed peas that lay fly-worried before them.

Not ten minutes before Linus Lancaster had corrected me about my respect, I had stood by those girls at their bath. Linus Lancaster said that anyone lived in his house would have a regular bath, and here they were at theirs. Zinnia had been pouring the water onto Cleome and the water had streamed off the bubbles Cleome had wiped onto herself. The bubbles had followed the water down Cleome's back and run white and ropey over her thighs and calves. She was bent and reaching for her towel when I slapped her. Then I slapped Zinnia. They both of them just looked at me. There wasn't anything beyond the bucket Zinnia was holding or I would have taken it to them. When I slapped Cleome I could feel that the water Zinnia had poured on her was cold. That they had pulled it up from the well.

From that dark hole in the earth. When I had my bath the water had been healed of its chill. One of the two of them heated it for me at the stove. One of them poured and the other took a cloth to me. There were bubbles on Cleome's ankles. She wasn't shivering. I found myself wanting to slap them again, so I did. I slapped until my hand hurt, and then I ran into the house and Linus Lancaster came down the corridor.

"Wife," he said.

I didn't answer. After he had pushed me hard enough that one of the boards in the door cracked he went and stood in the yard and watched Cleome and watched Zinnia who had gone back to their bath. My hand was still wet and soapy from where I had slapped Cleome. Linus Lancaster lit a pipe, looked at the girls, and I looked at my hand glistening and felt it burning in the hall.

None of us looked at Linus Lancaster when he put his spoon into his black-eyed peas and brought it up to his mouth then took a pull out of his bottle and turned and patted my hand and said it to me again. That I was the mother to them. Who would do worse than slap in the coming days. God help us all.

4.

WHEN WE WERE ALL STILL YOUNG in that place in Kentucky, and before the pigs had been set loose and the visits down the hall had commenced and I had become the mother to everyone there, we used to go out to where Alcofibras had his corner in the barn. We would go giggling out into the evening when Linus Lancaster was still at his work, whatever that was, far from the house and not expected back for supper, and we would find Alcofibras, and he would tell us stories that weren't out of that good book I never had found or out of any book I've ever known, and we would listen and sit together and shiver as he told them to us on the straw. Alcofibras had a voice that could churn as deep as a rock hole or high and twisty as a sick redbird, and he had had his stories from a grandmother who had come over in a boat. When he told his stories he never blinked. His eyes just flicked from one of us to the other. When he was finished we went back to whatever it was we had been doing or were supposed to be doing and needed to get done. We didn't giggle when he had completed his story.

We walked quietly. Sometimes Horace or Ulysses had come in with us for the telling. They were each one of them near as big as Linus Lancaster, but there wasn't any sound to them when they left either.

When they were young, I used to scrawl out stories to the children of my employer, Mr. Lucious Wilson, who had lost his wife when the second of them came into this world and looked to the ladies in his employ to ease the burden on him and his children's nurse. When it was my turn I would scrawl out stories I remembered from my burnt books about Rumpelstiltskin, that little man who spun gold and tore himself in half, and about Hansel and Gretel, who got themselves in a fix in that wood. I told them those stories and I told them others, but even though they came to call me Scary I never told them any of what we heard out in that barn from Alcofibras.

There was one about black bark and one about wet dough. In the one about black bark a man found a piece of black bark in his coat pocket and threw it away, but the next time he put on his coat it was there again. He threw that bark down a well and it was there again. He threw it into the fire and there it was. When he went to hit it with his hammer the piece of black bark opened its eye and looked at the man. Then it closed its eye, and the man lifted it up careful and put it in his pocket and never went anywhere without it again. In the one about wet dough, a woman was fixing to bake a pie. She got out her necessaries and rolled out her dough and put it into her dish. When she had it into her dish she looked at it and commenced to cry. The tears fell on the dough and the dough drank the tears until it could drink no more, and before long the tears had filled the dish. When they had filled the dish, the woman dried her eyes and took off her apron and walked out of the house and left that place forever. When the people who lived in the house with the woman came home, they found the pie dish and a piece of wet dough all curled up inside it like something drowned.

In another way Alcofibras told it, the woman never got to leave that place. She just cried and cried until everything wet in her had fallen into that dough and the dough drank it all and she just shriveled up and fell into pieces on the floor.

You hear something like that and it walks out the door with you. It follows you out the door to your work or your rest then jumps into your head and runs around inside it like a spider. You think there isn't much to a story like that and you think you've forgotten it, and a week later it is there. A year later it is there. Half a whole lifetime later it is there. Something like that gets in you and gets started and it doesn't stop. Alcofibras said his grandmother, who came over to this country with iron on her ankles like the iron you could find in Linus Lancaster's shed, could tell a story would put a nail through your foot. I had my stories from the grandson but didn't walk any better after them for that.

Last night I dreamed up I was sitting on a chair out in what's left of Lucious Wilson's barley field they've just harvested and didn't know what I was doing there and was about to holler out for one of the younger ones I used to tell Rumpelstiltskin stories to to come and harvest me out of there, when I tried to move my foot and couldn't and knew help or not this wasn't the running dream and I wasn't going anywhere.

"Come on out now, Alcofibras," I said.

"Taking my time, just like you," came his answer.

I could see him. Just as young and dark and fresh as he was when he was still drawing his breath.

Linus Lancaster did not like for Alcofibras to tell his stories to us, but that is not why he got taken to his end. It was one week not long after I'd been named mother to the brood, and Linus Lancaster had brought Horace and Ulysses on the two-day ride to the big town to sell off some of the pigs he'd set loose and had the devil's time herding up. He'd planned on just bringing Ulysses with him, but the pigs had turned ornery with their freedom and wouldn't walk straight without sufficient encouraging, so Linus Lancaster took Horace away with him too. That very same evening we had a visitor, and when Alcofibras came back on ahead of him down the lane he passed me and Cleome and Zinnia and said, "That's the Draper Man come to call." And when all three of us had cried out, he said, without slowing his step, "Not tonight, and ain't for you, that's the Draper Man for me."

The Draper Man was one of Alcofibras's stories about the man who comes to measure for the drapes, then has you step out the door with him to cut the cloth he will wrap you up in, then carries you off to your end. The man who came up the lane behind Alcofibras had on a top hat and purple britches. There were two of his help with him. I had Alcofibras take the help out to the barn and went inside the house with Mr. Bennett Marsden, as he said his name was, who was a friend of Linus Lancaster's from his days in Louisville when he had liked to sing on the stage. I had Zinnia, whom I had struck across the face that morning with the heavy spoon, see to supper, and I had Cleome, whom I had slapped across the back that afternoon with a switch of pig hide, fetch a bottle. They went to their jobs without any word to Bennett Marsden, who sat in Linus Lancaster's chair at the table and looked at them and said they had done grown up and transformed themselves into fillies.

"That Alcofibras ain't any more giant or any less ugly than he was, though," Bennett Marsden said when he had his soup and whiskey. "He still tell all those stories?"

"Have you heard Alcofibras's stories?"

"Tell you what, I'd like to hear another."

I sent the girls away and called for Alcofibras to come and stand by the table and tell a story to our guest. Alcofibras came in holding a potato in one hand and an onion in the other.

"Put those things outside and tell Mr. Bennett Marsden a story. He has asked for one," I said.

Alcofibras was quiet a long minute. He had a way of being quiet that cooked at your patience. I was fixing to correct him on it and for not taking the vegetables outside when his eyes flicked up at Bennett Marsden and he asked if he wanted to hear the story of the potato or the onion.

"Both," said Bennett Marsden with a laugh.

Alcofibras did not laugh, just let his eyes drop and went back into his quiet and stood there.

"Onion, then," said Bennett Marsden.

"He called for both," I said.

"Onion," said Alcofibras. He tossed the potato out into the yard and held up the onion. Then he went to the counter in the corner and took up the big knife sitting there and cut off its skin. When the onion was skinned he lifted it up and gave it a good sniff. There was some flour and bacon fat and corn pone and chopped apple and stewed oyster at the ready for Zinnia's cooking. Alcofibras took a little of each of these and set them in a line on the counter. Then he picked up the onion and turned to us again.

"The onion slept with a cord attached to its ankle in the coal cellar unless the coal cellar already had company and then he slept with a cord attached to his ankle in the yard. In the coal cellar the coal spoke to him, and in the yard it was the trees. One night the master came home with his face painted for the stage. The master lay about him until everything he struck had fallen. One did not rise and never would again, and when the master woke from his rage he wept, and before he had finished weeping the onion was gone. The oyster shell he had cut his cord with he kept along with a piece of bacon, a pocketful of flour, two apples, and a hunk of pone. He ran through the streets. His onion legs grew tired, so he took a bite of pone and made them strong. His onion arms and chest grew tired, so he took the oyster shell and cut the air in front of him and continued on. The city stretched before him. He ran toward the rising sun. A woman fetching water asked him why he was running, so he took a bite of one apple and turned her into an apple tree. Her child started to cry, so he took another bite and turned it into a buzzing bee.

"The onion ran and he ran. Near the outskirts a group of men set against him, so he broke off bits of the bacon and turned them into pigs. The pigs set into chasing after him, so he turned and cut at them with his shell. When they were killed he lit a fire and set a pot to boil and hung them over it and scraped them one by one. Then he butchered them and set some of them on skewers and caught their fat in a cup. He could hear barking, so he took off the cooled fat and carved it into a woman, and when he took a bite of his pone that woman blinked her eyes open and off together they ran.

"They ran but she was new to running and fell behind, so he turned her into a twig and put her in his pocket. The dogs came running after them, so he took some of the flour and flung it into the air and the air began to burn. The dogs ran through the fire and men came after them. They came and they came, so he flung more flour into the air and the air filled with water and the dogs drowned.

"When the dogs had drowned he took the twig out of his pocket and turned it back into his wife. They lay together on the mosses. They scratched their backs and fronts against the bark. They floated above the leaves. They had barely finished when his wife said, 'Here come some men.' The men carried torches. The onion took a bite of his other apple and the earth split asunder. The heavens raged and its powder kegs roared and a cataclysm ensued. The earth turned to water and the water to earth. Ice smashed at the trees. Time burned. There was a howl in the throat of the winds. Still the men came. He turned his wife into a stone and put her back in his pocket. He turned himself into a ball and went rolling and bouncing through the wood. It was dark, but the onion could see his way by the light of the torches behind him. Ever closer and ever brighter. The trees around him grew taller. They spoke to him. A door opened in one of them and he went into it.

"Inside the tree the sun was warm and there were soft grasses and a stream trickled by. There were sheep in the fields and flowers blooming and fat bees buzzed between them. An old man sat astride a mule and smiled down at the onion. 'You may stay here for ten years but must never ask for more,' he said, then rode away. The onion changed himself back into an onion and pulled the stone out of his pocket and made it into his wife again. 'We can live here for ten years.' 'Yes,' she said. They built a small house and planted a garden. They sat quietly together in the evenings. They lay down on soft blankets woven from cotton that grew wild in the hills. Once he tried to kill one of the sheep, but it scampered away laughing. So they ate that which they grew. By and by his wife had children. One after the other. The children poked sticks in the stream and played in the fields and tamed the sheep.

"When the ten years were almost up, the onion climbed onto one of the sheep and rode off in search of the man who had told them they could stay. He rode for weeks. Once he thought he saw the one he sought and called out to him to let his family stay. Immediately the onion became confused and could not find his way back to his house by the stream. His wife and children by the stream. Beneath him the sheep baaed and died and disap-peared. A cunning darkness crept up. The onion heard his master's laugh. It was hot in the hollow of the tree where the onion was hiding, and pig fat ran from his pocket. His apples were gone, his pone and bacon were gone, he had no oyster shell, his flour was soaked with fat.

"That night the onion slept in the coal cellar with iron on his ankle and his eyes shut from bruising. The next week the onion and his fellows rode out of Louisville in a procession. The onion wore a yoke and strained with the others to pull his master's wagon. He wore chains and was given nothing to eat."

"And what happened to the onion in the end?" Bennett Marsden said when Alcofibras had finished.

"I already showed you," Alcofibras said, holding up the skinned onion.

"So you did, so you did," said Bennett Marsden and roared, and I called for the girls to come back in and sent Alcofibras and his onion away again.

"Did you know my husband, Mr. Linus Lancaster, in Louisville, then?" I said after I had found my hosting voice, which had gotten lost in that wood with its pigs and sheep and furies.

"Yes, I knew him," Bennett Marsden said. He said this like it was something to say and laughed at the end of it. When he had finished his laugh, he said Alcofibras hadn't lost any of his storytelling style, and I asked him which of Alcofibras's stories he had heard, told him "Black Bark" and "Wet Dough" were my favorites, but he didn't respond, just looked far away for a while, then asked me for some of

Linus Lancaster's tobacco. I sent Cleome out to fetch it. When she was back with it the kitchen seemed crowded, so I sent her away. Bennett Marsden watched her go out the door. When he had started up his smoking, he pushed his hat back on his head and pointed over at Zinnia, who was stirring her oyster and apple concoction at the long table by the wall.

"I knew the mother to that one and the other too. There was about twice as much to her in terms of dimension, physically speaking, as to either one of these, but she had a pretty face like they do."

"Was she also in my husband's service?"

"That's one way to sum it up."

"And did she pass?"

"It was the fever took her off is the story got told. A bad gust. She wasn't the only one that fever struck down."

Zinnia did not turn when he said this. She did not stop stirring the soup either. Bennett Marsden then showed us a trick about how he could pull his lips back and put his spoon into his mouth through the teeth he was missing on one side. He laughed at his own trick, and I laughed too. Then he turned and asked, though there wasn't much question to it, if I was the new lady of the house. I reckoned he was looking at me and thinking of Linus Lancaster's dearly departed, so I straightened up and smoothed my skirt in my lap and asked him if he had known that lady who had preceded me. He gave me a kind of squint when I asked this, then gave it over at Zinnia, then squinted at me again. Then he called over to Zinnia for another spoon

and showed us how the trick could be done with two at
once.

"Yes ma'am, I knew her," he said when he had completed his trick.

Bennett Marsden laughed his laugh and drank, and the
evening found some tolerable way to complete itself. When
we had him into Linus Lancaster's bed, I asked Zinnia to
explain the poor consideration she had tended toward a
friend of Linus Lancaster's from the old days, and she didn't
answer, just looked down at me, so I hit her on the side of
the head with the wooden bowl I was holding and she
went down on one big knee and stayed there bleeding until
I told her to get up.

The next morning Bennett Marsden said he couldn't
wait for Linus Lancaster, but that I should extend his kind-
est regards and memories of the olden days and their business dealings together, especially their business dealings
together, the good and the bad. Then he and his two help
left back down the lane, and I told Alcofibras that his
Draper Man had come and gone and he ought to feel just
like a fool for calling him that and for inventing tall tales
about pig fat and magic trees, but Alcofibras would not
answer. He walked away, and as he walked away another
one of his stories came to me. There wasn't much to it. It
was about a piece of red rope. The whole of the story was
that sometimes that piece of red rope lying there without
anybody to touch it would move.

Two days later Linus Lancaster came home, and when
he heard that his old friend from Louisville, Bennett

Marsden, had come to call and had spent the night in his bed, he tied Alcofibras to the oak tree by the barn and whipped him until his back was a sheet of crimson cloth.

We all of us were directed to form up a line and look on while the whipping of Alcofibras was conducted. I had first place in the line because of my standing. Horace and Ulysses stood next to me and Zinnia and Cleome were at the end. Not a one of them said a word. Linus Lancaster had explained to me that Alcofibras should have never let that Bennett Marsden onto the property when he wasn't there. That Bennett Marsden was a liar and a disreputable individual and should have never been granted access to his piece of paradise while he, Linus Lancaster, was abroad. I was excused from the matter because I had never known that filthy cheat Bennett Marsden in the old days as Alcofibras had. I should have known better than to let anyone into the house when he wasn't there, and should have been able to judge the quality of the character of the man I had let sleep in his bed and smoke up his tobacco, but it was Alcofibras had to answer.

As that whipping went on you could hear pigs they hadn't sold off at it in the dusk light at the corners of everything, and out over the field you could see tornadoes of evening birds harrowing the insects.

"You must stop now, Husband," I whispered at one point. I know the four of them next to me heard this. I also know that Linus Lancaster did not.

When Alcofibras was dead of the crimson cloth on his back, Linus Lancaster had Horace and Ulysses carry him out to the woods for the pigs we had been hearing, but I know that when Horace and Ulysses got Alcofibras out there they took sticks and scraped a hole and buried him and covered the place with rocks so the pigs couldn't dig him up.

That night, as I lay there in my room while Linus Lancaster paid his visits, I couldn't conjure up any daisy fields. I couldn't conjure up any castles in the clouds or lemonade. I couldn't see my way back to my father's house with its goose pond and my corner bed. It was just lengths of red rope, rope that shouldn't be moving, rope untouched that was slithering over the walls and windows, filling my mouth and apron pockets, wrapping field and flower, tree and bush, bird and pig.

5.

SNOW IS COME UP ON Lucious Wilson's barley field. It falls just every other day now and the wind has taken some of it up over the fence rows. There were some stray dogs through yesterday, and they just walked up over one fence and across the snows of the field and up over the other. I haven't seen them before. They looked like they had business. I'm happy for this little house. I wouldn't ever say otherwise. The stove works and heats these old boards. A crack or two court the drafts, but there are hay bales and paper wad to talk to that.

Before I came up into the flat country here and found Lucious Wilson and his farm, I lived in other accommodations. In Spencer County I lived under some boards stretched across an old dogwood. I lived there until I woke up one morning next to a snake attempting to swallow down a rat. In Evansville I had a pallet next to a gun rack. It was a brother and a sister owned the place and sold charms and remedies out of their kitchen. One night I wandered in my sleep and upset one of their buckets. The oil

covered the kitchen floor and swept its wet way into the
front room where they slept. I'd seen the sister kick a slow
goat in its teeth. I didn't stay to have any of my own kicked
out. When I got my way up to Indianapolis I lived in a
closet down by the capitol building, and my first week up
here, until one of Lucious Wilson's women found me, I
lived my nights in a cold frame attached to an outhouse. I
don't care to count this second how many years ago that
was. Lucious Wilson is old now too, and there are the others who call me Scary Sue come up under him and are
waiting for him to go. I told them stories when they were
young and gave them baths, and they some of them look
in on me, but charity passed to the next generation has its
limits, and I'm counting on being gone before Lucious
Wilson heads out on his way.

It is cold here in Clinton County, Indiana, far up away
from Linus Lancaster's piece of paradise in Kentucky is all
I was saying. And that there aren't many lately of the young
ones who come to the house and holler. They tried to get
me over to church last week, but I slipped on the walk and
two of them had to carry me back into the house. About
the last time anyone got carried into this house was during
the war. It was some soldiers got lost and drunk, and one
of them caught a fever and fell off his horse. A little like
Lucious Wilson's pig herder. The battle guns were still a-
blazing off somewhere, so Lucious Wilson said they ought
to carry him into this little house until he could get back
up on his horse and rejoin the festivities. I was still living
in the big house then, but I brought him over a supper one

night. He was a handsome boy. He had green eyes and fine red lips and little curls in his beard. There have been times even into these older days I've enjoyed remembering his face and long arms lying down in the bed that's just right there behind me. That bed and mattress where I have spent all the nights of these years. There wasn't much wrong with that boy except being young and wore out on fighting.

I know that there was snow in between what came next in that place in Kentucky and that visit from the Draper Man, but in my mind I just take one little step over the dead Alcofibras, and one little step over myself where Linus Lancaster had beat me down half dead the next week for asking what business he had been in with Mr. Bennett Marsden in Louisville, and a hop over Cleome and Zinnia and the dark thing that had recommenced nightly visiting them, to that knock on my door early that morning that interrupted a dream I had been busy having about grinding chicory for a breakfast drink.

There was a knock and then some talking, then the door opened fast and both girls came in. They took me up out of my bed and pulled me through the door and down the hall past their own door and into the kitchen. They sat me at a chair opposite my husband. It was dark in the kitchen. And cold. My husband looked to be sleeping. Like he had been up the night drinking his drink and had just settled out where he sat. Cleome turned up the lamp and Zinnia went behind Linus Lancaster and shoved him and he came down onto the table and his face dropped down through the lamplight, and you saw before you saw the pig sticker in the back of his neck when his face dropped down through the light that there wasn't going to be any more singing or visiting and whippings come from him. The face was as white as a piece of china plate, and you could see the veins of it writhing in the lamp flicker like worms a-swarm in milk soup. The mouth was open like he was preparing to cough, and his eyes were looking up and over to the right. The hairs that lived in his nose grazed down through the lamplight too. They looked like they were try-ing to jump out overboard. Like hooked hands going down to drown.

"You must have your breakfast now, Mother," Cleome said after my husband's head had hit down on the table opposite me and I had been permitted to consider it for a time. The pig sticker in his neck looked like a thick-stem flower that had had its head lopped off. Like it had had its head lopped off but not yet set in to droop.

"I aim to get you up some of that pig mush, fix you up just right now," Cleome said. There were sundries on the board behind her. A small fire in the stove. Zinnia nodded. There was sweat on her forehead. It looked like her face was bubbling, like it was porridge fixing to depart the pot. The room was still cold.

"I don't care to take my breakfast just now, Cleome," I said.

"It's already cooking," said Cleome.

"It's already cooking, Mother," said Zinnia.

"I have spoken," I said. "We must tend . . . We must . . ."

"We must what, Mother?" Zinnia said. She said this in a whisper from just behind me. I hadn't seen her move. Cleome had stopped working the mush but was still looking down to it through the spit from the fat and the orange steam. I couldn't remember ever having seen her at the stove for anything more than serving before.

"I don't know," I said.

I put my hands on the table in front of me and Zinnia put her hand on my shoulder, and it felt exactly like I was trying to stand myself up under a piece of iron bar. Zinnia had on that hat Linus Lancaster had put her in the shed over those years before. She had been in that shed many times since. I had put her in that shed. I had put Cleome in that shed. I had put them both in there since Linus Lancaster had thrown me down onto the floor out of his bed and had set in to visiting them. Visiting them while they dreamed of anything but twisting daisies with me. I had put them both in there since Alcofibras had been fitted for his drapes by Mr. Bennett Marsden. I had stood in the sunlight of the doorway and told them I was going to drop the key to their shackle down the well. Zinnia leaned her face down around in front of mine and there was the sweat bubbling on her brow, and I thought I could see myself in each dull black bead, and Cleome came up next to her and took the hat off of her sister's head and put it down on mine.

"You going to eat your breakfast now, Mother," Zinnia said.

"Where is Horace? Where is Ulysses?" I said.

"Run off. Run off far away. Gone from this place. Ain't never coming back," said Zinnia.

Cleome set down an empty bowl, an empty spoon, and an empty cup in front of me.

Then Zinnia picked them up, one by one, and fed them to me.

Now let me tell of my four-square kingdom. At one corner of it was the barn where Alcofibras had dwelled and spun out his stories and the oak tree where he had been whipped into the other world. At another was the miserable house where I had lived for six years and where Linus Lancaster had paid his visits and been lord to us all, and where he now sat royal and dead. At the third was the little bridge to the creek-lipped field Horace and Ulysses had put in where once there had been pasture for horses and where I had once frolicked at my ease with those around me, and where now the pigs liked to come down out of the wood and lay down their huge carcasses and roll and tumble like flippered creatures on some black beach at the edge of hell. At the fourth was the shed with its chain and its rats. In the middle of it was the deep well we pulled our water up out of and dropped rocks down into when it froze. All around us were the woods. Through the woods went the lane. Down that lane my figment self would trot. Up into the leaf-lit sky my figment self would rise. Into the black Kentucky earth my figment self would sink. Down the well and past the dangling ghost of young Cleome and out through the endless waters of the earth my figment self would swim.

The flesh part, the blood part stayed put. Here is why. After that breakfast and after they had poured a bucket of water over my head to wake me up, and put Zinnia's pig-slop hat back on my head, they dragged me out to the shed and put the shackle on my leg and told me to rest up awhile. That while was three days and three nights. After the second night Zinnia walked in with a bowl of water, and when I grabbed for it, she kicked it over then walked back out. After the third night they had me back into the house to breakfast again with my husband. There was food to it this time. My husband lay like he had. His hair was spilled forward. The rats had found their way in at him. He hadn't been able to fight them like I had. Hadn't been able to wake from his sorry sleep and shake a chain at them, toss a kick at them. Zinnia put foodstuff and water before me and told me to eat, or I'd have another breakfast like the last one. I ate. I had a cracked tooth or two but I ate. Cleome sat on the bench outside while I did so. I heard her say to Zinnia she would not set her foot again in that house. They had laid down their blankets in the barn. To sleep where Alcofibras had. Among the animals. Where it was clean.

I ate and imagined my punishment was complete. That my children would now bathe me and put poultices on the bruises they had administered to me and return to their rightful places. That I would take them each by the hand and lead them off down the lane on an outing that would end in the sun somewhere, with peppermint and licorice and sugar candy and a peek at a Chinaman sitting in a black barrel. I looked at Linus Lancaster as I imagined this, and in my looking saw him raise his head up off the table and point the pig sticker at the flour sack behind him and start to sing. He sang "Glory, Hallelujah" as I ate and looked. By and by Zinnia grabbed me up by my scruff and took me out to the oak tree.

"For some seasoning, Mother," Cleome said, lifting up off her bench. When she lifted you could see clear as crisp-light the condition all that visiting from Linus Lancaster had put her in.

"Keep that old hat on your head while we cook you, Mother," said Zinnia.

"Stand up straight now, Mother."

"Please don't have nothin' to do with it, Mother."

"The woods will eat all that hollerin', Mother."

"You can cry out those tears later, Mother."

"Cryin' don't help with a thing when that thing is set on coming to pass."

I breakfasted with my husband all the days following. After
the first week Zinnia made me get my own breakfast while
she and Cleome waited together on the bench outside.
When I wasn't in there getting and having my breakfast,
which was the only meal I got each day, they kept the
doors to Linus Lancaster's house closed so that nothing
beside the rats could get in there after him. The pigs, I
believe they reckoned, would have made too quick a job.

I don't know what it was they discussed while I was at
my breakfast. It may not have been much. There was never
a good deal of talking between them. Even when we were
all younger. There had never been a great deal of discussion
between my husband, Linus Lancaster, and myself, so that
hadn't changed much with the situation either. He had liked
to talk at me a fair amount, and I had listened as he did so
and looked to my work. So to keep a sense of balance where
there was none any longer, I talked at him now during those
breakfasts while Cleome and Zinnia waited outside on the
bench, and while he listened and looked to the work of
being dead as a doorstopper. I talked at his forehead, which
was ever dripping forward and pooling up on the table and
sogging toward the edges and spooling toward the floor, and
I talked at his hair, which had a blue sheen on it that had
probably settled down from the stink stuck to the dust that
had always been in that air. I talked to his shoulders and his
brown, heavy cloth shirt, and his big hands glowing yellow
and purple and gray in the kitchen light.

At first it was just things about whippings and being
beat and the nothing work they'd set me to that came out

of my mouth like the thought that runs a black garble through a mind and can pass, if you petition it kind enough to, for anything you ever hoped it could be. Then I told him about how he had never ought to have come up to my father's house in Indiana and fetch me. How he ought to have left me to my corner in that house and to my church up there above the river, where there had been other Christians to commune with and where they hadn't minded if every now and again I would sing.

"I have a pretty voice," I said to my husband.

"You never built your big house with its fifty-foot porch and its wide staircases and its columns and gables," I said to him.

"Look at you dead now," I said. "When you took us all to that carnival in Albatross, you ought to have let me have those stockings I saw or brought back Cleome and Zinnia that bag of candy. You ought never to have whipped Alcofibras, let alone until he was dead. You ought never to have started your visiting down the hall or taken your boot to me in your bed. A pig is a filthy thing and here I am still eating it for my breakfast, and how, husband, do you like how your dream about the greensward turned out?"

I said these things to my husband with the pig sticker in his neck, and the house beyond him no longer seemed like it had anything to do with me or the six years of my life it had bitten the head off, and I crunched my breakfast and when I came out into the light and fresh air, Cleome and Zinnia would be waiting. At the first days, Zinnia would take me by the arm or the scruff, but after a time she would just shove me on along in front and the two of them would follow me out to wherever they had set my chore for the day. One morning it was mowing spring grass with the hand sickle. Another it was clearing rocks. I thought once or twice that I could have run away from Cleome, but Zinnia was like hell with wings, and no matter what lead I could have conjured, she would have chased me down and smashed my bones to powder. Even when Linus Lancaster had laid his hands on me I had never felt so infirm. Zinnia was all quiet, then all noise. Like it was coming out with her sweat, clouding into steam.

Once, after they had left aside the regular chores and settled into making me dig holes—as deep as my head, then fill it up and start again—Zinnia leapt down into the hole with me and hit me with her fists and elbows until they had to haul me out of there with a rope. This was the hole I should have had dug for Alcofibras she said as they hauled me up. This was the hole would have kept him soft and safe and quiet, not left to the snakes and cold winds under a blanket of rocks.

"You can keep digging holes until your hands fall off, Mother," she said.

"I will," I said.

"I know you will."

"I'll never stop."

"No, you won't."

"First my fingers will fall off, then my hands, then my wrists, then my elbows, then the rest of my arms."

"And you will still keep digging."

"Yes."

For her part, Cleome got quieter as her time passed. Her small face grew wider and her eyes larger, and her hair fell with fresh oils that caught the sunlight.

I would tell Linus Lancaster about all this at our breakfasts together. I would eat pork and mush and look at his dead forehead and talk at him about how the angel he had carried on his shoulder sat on Zinnia's shoulder now and about how quiet Cleome was and how there was a sweetness somewhere sipping at that quiet and how far she had gotten along.

Sometimes I picked up my talking at the end of the day when I was lying on the dirt floor of the shed. It wasn't unusual that my lips were too cracked to move nice enough for real talk, so I would just run it in my head. Linus Lancaster, you are dead and I am lying out here with a shackle on my ankle, and Cleome is grown bigger and bigger, and Zinnia is fixing to strike me down so I won't come up again. The rats are in there at you, and then they'll come out and look to me, and everything they ever sang in those old songs about the hard places a body can come to are true.

But the cold dark is a fretful place to pose a colloquy, even if it is just in your head. So mostly I just lay there. Waiting for my breakfast. Looking out for the rats. Without any more dainties about outings and candy and Chinamen in barrels and daisies and such. My arms still digging into the black and rock of the earth, even though it had been hours since they had in the actuality stopped. Counting, as

my arms still dug, as I waited for them to fall off, on the
pig sticker or any one of its evil cousins to come for me
and swallow me up.

6.

WHEN LUCIOUS WILSON'S WOMAN had me out of the cold frame behind the outhouse and into the light, she did not lift the heavy stick she had taken up at me and she did not ask me any question about how I had come to be there. She was an old woman and had an eye to see through things, and she saw through my skin where it had healed or it hadn't to the wounds I had lately had, and through those to the wounds I had offered unto others, and through those to that four-square kingdom in Kentucky and the woods that surrounded it and the thundering tunnel of my days that led up to my father's house in Indiana where I had started out from. She looked at me and she blinked her crop-colored eyes and dropped her heavy stick and told me wherever I'd been, I couldn't live in Lucious Wilson's cold frame and I'd better come on.

Lucious Wilson didn't have that old woman's eye, but he had that old woman, and after she had nodded, he told me there was a place for me in his employ if I knew how to work and wanted it, and I told him I did. He did not

ask me where I had come from. I expect that after she had
gotten me bathed and settled the old woman had told him.
Whether or not her seeing extended to the naming part of
things, she told me that first night they would need to
know what to call me. I thought of my old teacher and told
her that my name was Sue.

"Well, Sue, you aren't sleeping in a cold frame tonight
or any night after if that's the way you want it," she said.

"That's the way I want it," I said.

The next weekend they had me over to a revival outside of town where there was a line-up for dunking, and
that old woman had me take my place. The minister spoke
and dunked and spoke again. It was a pretty place, and
they had set up garlands on the bushes. The spot they were
in was next to a short bridge and the little ones had their
legs dangling off it. Lucious Wilson went in the front of us.
He had on a fine suit and waded right out into the water
and let the minister speak his words and dunk him down.
There were some of his other folk in the line, men and
women, then there was me. I had on some Sunday clothes
they'd given me. There were good folks on the banks, all
dripping and weeping and wiping at the air above their
faces with their hands.

"Go on now, Sue," the old woman said.

I went. I stepped into the water and the water, which
the minister had been telling could be robe and belt both
to any who wanted it, walked away to either side of me. I
stepped on the bottom and as I stepped, the water walked
even away out of the mud and my borrowed shoes kept

dry. The minister spoke his words about salvation and the blood of the good lamb and leaned me back and pushed me down, but the water had walked away, and when I came up I was dry. I know the minister knew this because when he spoke his words again about the robe and the belt, he whispered them up against my ear and never when he was finished with his whispering said amen, and I know the old woman knew because when I got back out onto the bank, she said the best thing to do about it would be to sit on the grass by the garlanded bushes with the others and, dry or wet, commend myself to Him who was lurking everywhere. To Him who sat in the shadows and the dark parts with us. To Him who would in the end harrow every evil and offer even those of us the water didn't want, and whom the water wasn't helping, a jewel from his glittering crown.

That's not what Alcofibras came back to tell me. All those weeks after Linus Lancaster had been pushed down onto the table, Alcofibras didn't walk through the wall of my enshackled night to sit cross-legged and ringed by rats before me and commune about robes and jewels and crowns. After he had sat, shrunk and whip-broken, lit by the glow of his own burning eyes, wrapped in a red shawl, he hadn't stood himself up to speak about the coming of the Lord. I know that, even though all he said to me by way of greeting in that bowl of blackness was, "Evenin', Miss Ginny." No one, not even me with one of my eyes shut to bruising, would have mistaken what followed for anything to do with the lamb.

Alcofibras flung back that shawl and showed out his whip-cut shoulders and lifted up his gangle legs and twisted his arms, and the light from his eyes lit up every bit of him. His knees went up either side higher than his head, and the pink soles of his feet slapped back down on the ground. There wasn't any music to it beside those pink soles slapping the cold ground. Presently his hands commenced to hit together. When they had come back away from each other, he would hold them out at me like he was saying *Stop.* Then he bowed and showed his back and shoulders then threw up his eyes at me. Then he bowed again and pulled his shawl over his head and shuffled around until his naked back was before me, then he raised up and leaned this way around, and as I looked an eye the size of a saucer opened up in the middle of his shoulders then closed, and he turned and pulled his shawl back down and smiled at me and recommenced lifting his legs and slapping his soles and hitting his hands and holding them out like he was saying *Stop*.

Then he stood still and looked at me, and looked at me and looked at me, and mouths grew up over his arms and legs and each one of them opened and all of them wailed at once, then went closed and quiet. Alcofibras then came up closer to me, his knees climbing to either side of him and his hands hitting together, and he leaned in close and when he did, ears came out of his forehead and his cheeks and his neck and his chest, until they were on every part of him and even the ears had grown ears and the ears were shaking, and I found myself sobbing because all they had to listen to was my poor breath and my poor heart, and all his mouth had had to wail to and all that eye had had to look upon was my poor self, shackled in the dark, a sorry thing of the earth, when outside there was so much, when out beyond my four-square kingdom, out along the midnight flanks of the republic, out atop the great wide oceans there was so much, and I called out to Alcofibras, who after a hundred, a thousand years was sitting quiet again with the shawl wrapped around his shoulders and his own dead eyes and ears and mouth, "What have you shown me?"

"What I showed to your father when we stood out there in the woods that day you come up on us and hid behind a tree."

"And what was that?"

"The way of the World, Mother. The way of the World, Miss Ginny," he said.

I did not breakfast with my husband the following morning. Nor did I break my bread with him the morning after
that nor any over the week to come. I sat or lay in that
shed, and they did not come to get me to dig holes and fill
holes or hug at the oak tree. They kept the door open during the long day, and when I was able, I leaned against the
boards at the back of the shed and looked out at the well
and the woods beyond. Now and again a pig would wander past. One rainy afternoon a sow came in out of the wet
and curled up in the corner, and I passed some hours in
contemplating the mud on her fat flank and the lift and fall
of her midsection and the kick she would give when she
hit some rough pasture in her dream. When she woke she
walked over to me and gave me a sniff.

"Yes, I would like to kill you and grind you and eat
you," I said.

"Go on and try," she said.

"I would get a big skillet and set the whole of you in
it," I said.

"Only I would get a big skillet and set the whole of you
in it first, and then I would call in my youngins and let
them set their sloppy mouths to you first," she said.

"Yes," I said.

"Yes," she said.

Then she flicked her tail and walked off.

Once or twice over that week I woke on my dirt to
find a bowl of water and some dry cornbread next to me,
but I never saw my benefactors. They had turned themselves into voices, and those voices would come and sit on

the other side of the boards behind me and speak or sing. On the fourth day I lost track of what it was they would sing or say. On the fifth day I spoke and sang back, but each time I did the voices went away to the land where voices live in columns of wind and light. On the following day, they did not. They remained there on the other side of the boards. So I sang them "Glory, Hallelujah" and "The Old Wooden Cross." I sang them "The Star-Spangled Banner" and a yuletime song I didn't know the name of. There wasn't much lung to my voice, but it came out.

When I didn't have any song to sing I talked. I told them I'd seen Alcofibras dancing, and that he might be back to dance some more just any one of the nights to come. I told them that after he had come to dance for me he had come into one of my dreams and torn pieces of himself off to eat until all that was left was his mouth. I told them otherwise I'd been thinking about the stars in the sky and the cold proposition they presented, for I had. I told them I'd been thinking about the wind in the big trees and the animals clinging to their branches, for I had. I told them I'd scraped myself out a long, low pit to sleep my nights in and that I was grateful for the blanket they had given me and for the slops and the water, for I was. I told them I had been thinking about old Pharaoh and the Egyptians and the jasmine and brook flowers and amethysts he had worn against his breast, and how when I was a child I had often wished to lay my eyes on all the glories of Earth's kingdom as well as heaven's, for this was true.

I told them that when Linus Lancaster had come up to Indiana in the long ago, he had not come with it in his mind to fetch me, that he had come with another in mind. He had come up to fetch his second cousin, my mother. He had got word that my father had lost life along with limb in his battle and was in the hereafter with all the dearly departeds of the earth, and he came knowing that his second cousin, my mother, had always favored him. I told them I knew this because I had heard my father and my mother yelling over it. My father was for putting Linus Lancaster out into the yard on his ignorant ear. There were ways to confirm whether someone was deceased or just crippled before you came calling after what had or hadn't been left behind.

I told my benefactors beyond the wall that after I had heard this fight and understood Linus Lancaster's errand, I had twirled myself up in front of him, thinking in my foolishness that I wanted to be quit of my father's house and my father's cane, and had sat down on Linus Lancaster's broad lap under an apple tree and made him look my way, and that I had said soft things about his dearly departed and had blown heat into his heart even though I knew nothing about heat nor about heart. That I had bought up in advance every crumb of the loaf that had been baked for me and now was eating it. For I had and I was.

I told them all of this and sat up against the board and shivered and wiped sweat from my brow and looked out the open door to the well and all the holes I had dug and filled to the big woods beyond, where what was left of Alcofibras lay buried under rocks in his bloody shawl.

"I'd like to come out now and walk to the woods," I told them.

"Aren't you out here with us already?" said one of the voices.

"Aren't you out here with us right now?" said the other.

Yes, I thought. I am.

For I was.

I went floating past them where they sat on their bench. I floated across the yard and into the barn and out through one of its windows. I passed the sow I had previously parlayed with. I skittered along the surface of the creek. There were fish in its soft currents. I floated and floated. Then a wind came up and took me at my throat and flung me back into my dark.

7.

YOU WOULD HAVE THOUGHT that spring would be here by now, but I look out my window and there the snow still sits. They had me out to church again after several weeks this past Sunday, and after the singing and such the minister told us about Isaac and his son. I expect I was not the only one in the pews who thought, Here we go again with Isaac. It is one of the stories they like to tell. And as for that it is better than some. The burning bush is a choice touch. It is something you can see and believe in when they talk. It puts an image in the mind that will spit and scorch. After you leave the church and you have heard that story, it is hard not to look at every bush you pass a little crosswise. Even little spindly things all crushed up in the snow. Lucious Wilson and his people use sleighs to get to church when the snow is deep, and after church they loaded me into one of the sleighs and set off for home. I like a sleigh ride. That is one thing I never lost the pleasure of. I know I am not alone in it. The Draper Man made a remark to that effect on his second visit to my late husband's piece of Kentucky paradise.

"I like a good sleigh ride, don't you?" he said.

"Sliding and whooshing over the white world," I said.

He came after they had pulled me out of that shed and stood me up in the basin and poured well water and soap bubbles over me until I was clean. They didn't do it soft or rough. They just did it. When it was done they took me naked into the house, through the empty kitchen and into what had been my bedroom, and had me take down a dress and pull it over my head. Then they took me back to the kitchen and sat me down in my chair and worked the brush through my hair. They worked and worked and in other times I might have cried for it. Now I just waited and watched. When they were done and my wet hair was sitting on my back and shoulders like something come in from a wig shop, they put a wedge of salt pork in front of me and a cup of cider out of a barrel they'd found in the barn. The kitchen had been cleaned and they had on their old aprons, and there was a minute when I got to thinking that I'd blink and Linus Lancaster would walk in like it all never was through the door.

"Where is he?" I said.

"Where is who?" Cleome said.

"Linus Lancaster."

"Gone," Zinnia said.

"Gone off to his heaven."

"He in his reward."

"Sweetmeats for his pigs."

"You dug the hole but we put Alofibras in it instead."

I ate. I did not look at them as I did so. Neither did I speak anymore. By and by Zinnia put more pork before me and told me to eat it up. She said a pair of red Indians, a man and his woman, had come out of the wood and walked straight up to them and told them to expect a visitor. She had showed those Indians Linus Lancaster's old gun and they had walked away back into the woods, but that night she had dreamed it up that they were there again and talking again, only this time they said who they meant.

"Draper Man's comin' back," Zinnia said.

"When?" I said.

"Don't know. Dream didn't say. But when he gets here, Ginny, you will stand up straight and be the mother to us again."

He came the next day down the lane with just one man this time, but otherwise with his top hat and purple britches like before. Zinnia was the one to go out and meet him. Cleome took me out of the shed and into the house while she did this. When Bennett Marsden got up to the yard, he took off his hat and bowed.

"I have come back in hopes of a parlay with your husband," he said.

"My husband is away again."

"Ah," he said.

"And taken Ulysses and Horace away again with him."

"Ah," he said again. He looked around. "And that Alcofibras and his onion?"

"Deceased. Last autumn after your leaving."

"I lost one of mine too. Pox took him during the snows. Did it come here and importune you?"

"Yes it did."

Bennett Marsden sent his man to the barn and came into the kitchen, and we fetched up food and drink and placed the start of it down before him.

"You have been poorly, Mrs. Lancaster," he said, looking me up and down.

"I have been unwell, yes," I said.

"Was it the fever? The fever is a harsh master. It will smite you down."

"It was an inconvenience, yes. But I'm mending now."

I had taken my seat at the table and had twice reached for its surface to steady me and twice missed it. What color is the world when you can't see it any longer? I had thought the second time. What is the smell of lobelia when they have removed your nose? How does a horse flank feel to your fingers when they have chopped off your hand? There was an awkwardness to all three of us. Cleome huffed in a corner and worked at the meat. Zinnia stirred away like she had before, only I knew, because they had told me how it would be, that she had the pig sticker from Linus Lancaster's neck in her apron pocket. Bennett Marsden had taken his hat off upon entering the kitchen. His hair was greased up from his hat and his dirty fingers so it looked like three quarters of a crow's wing had fallen out of the blue sky and smacked him on his head.

"Will you favor us with one of your tricks, Mr. Marsden?" I said.

Bennett Marsden smiled and told us he would entertain us presently. He had a tooth or two fewer in his mouth than he'd had before.

"Did you know your husband, Mr. Lancaster, and I were on the stage together in Louisville?" he said.

"I did not know that."

"He was the center of it. He'd sing out his lines and they'd all sit tight. I got up there afterward and kind of clowned around. Not much talent to it. I'd clown and recite. This was recreational. Not neither one of our central remunerative lines."

"Is that a fact?" I said.

"We had thoughts about making it otherwise, but they didn't come to pass."

"Didn't they?"

"That one's expecting," Bennett Marsden said, holding out his cup to Cleome, who had ceased belaboring the meat and passed it over to Zinnia, who was leaning against the counter looking over at us. She pushed herself off the counter, carried the bottle to Bennett Marsden, and filled his cup.

"She is encumbered, yes," I said.

"Encumbered," Bennett Marsden said.

This was the way my father had liked to say it I had never become encumbered, and Linus Lancaster had put his boot in my back and never had me back into his bed. I could see, from where I sat at the kitchen table, the door to the room where Cleome and Zinnia had received their visits. My own door was somewhere farther off down in the dark.

"Well, nature will find its ways to multiply," Bennett Marsden said with a fat, wet smack of his lips. Then he finished his cup, called Zinnia over for another, then said

we could now have our trick and should prepare ourselves
for something with more spectacle to it than the previous
time, something that would hold the mind as well as
Alcofibras's story had. He pushed up from the table,
smoothed down his crow's wing, hunched his shoulders
over, and turned a handstand right there at my dead husband's kitchen table. Then he walked around the kitchen,
past me, past Cleome, past Zinnia, and then around again
and twice more. As he did this, I reflected on Zinnia's pig
sticker and the shallow hole that was waiting for me in my
shed. They seemed like one thing in my mind. More and
more as the trick went on. While our guest ran upside
down around that kitchen he recited.

> All the infections that the sun sucks up
> From bogs, fens, flats, on Prosper fall, and make him
> By inch-meal a disease! His spirits hear me,
> And yet I needs must curse.
> Sometime like apes that mow and chatter at me
> And after bite me, then like hedgehogs which
> Lie tumbling in my barefoot way and mount
> Their pricks at my footfall

After his performance, which I clapped for, Bennett
Marsden drank and told me that my husband, Linus
Lancaster, owed him enough money to sink a Spanish ship
out of the old stories, and that he aimed to have it from him.

"Does that seem inopportune or incourteous to you,.
madam?" he asked me.

"No," I said. "It seems fair."

"Fair indeed," he said. "When do you expect him?"

I watched Zinnia's back stiffen and Cleome's swollen midsection rise up and flop when Bennett Marsden asked this.

"My husband, Linus Lancaster, does not tell me such things," I said.

"Well enough and true enough, I expect," said Bennett Marsden.

"Yes, it is true," I said.

After I had said this Zinnia came over to the table with a plate of fried pork swimming in molasses and put it down in front of our guest.

"It's minutes like these I thank the dear Lord he's left me teeth enough to chew," Bennett Marsden said

"Zinnia's cooking is truly a blessing," I said. I said this without any playacting. I'd forgotten for that five seconds who or what I was. I had always commented on Zinnia's cooking. Even in those days when I was taking the strop to her for no crime but being candy with her sister to that dead husband of mine.

That night I slept in my old room and Cleome and Zinnia in theirs. There were all my things. My chest of notions. My little vase with dead stalks in it. My frocks and dresses hanging like leftover slab meat from pegs on the wall. Bennett Marsden, lying in Linus Lancaster's old bed, had a snore could crack a coffin lid. A body could offer evil to a man who snored that loud. Whether or not he could turn on his hands and sing out pretty about monkeys and hedgehogs.

But at that moment there wasn't any evil or much else in my body to offer. So there I lay breathing my breaths. Linus Lancaster came to visit me that night. He stood at the end of my bed with the pig sticker borrowed out of Zinnia's apron pocket and put back in his neck.

"Have you come to dance for me, Husband?" I said.

He shook his head. His eyes had a glow to them. He looked smaller than he had in life. There were no ears or eyes on his arms. He wore no crimson cape. After a time he cleared his dead throat and said he would tell his side of the tale of the dealings between him and Bennett Marsden and made the following speech:

"We went in halves to build a grand theater, Bennett Marsden and I, but I borrowed my half from him and he borrowed his half from me. We thought there was considerable good jest in this and sat down to our fresh partnership with the laugh of it still on our lips. We had our drink in the good old Louisville Belle, then walked down the street to what he thought we ought to call the Flourish and what I thought we ought to call the World. We stood outside it when it was close to finished, him calling it his name and I calling it mine. There was work aplenty to do before we had to put a name up over the doors, time and more for me to make sure the name to it was mine.

"Well, Wife, we did that work with each of us in his shirtsleeves and sweating the same sweat. We'd each put in two of our creatures to the job, and even though mine were bigger and better in all ways, I couldn't fault his that they took after him, nor credit mine for taking after me. At the

end of the sweeping and the dusting and the breaking
down and the building up each day we would drink at the
Belle or send out for a bottle. Then, with drink in our bel-
lies, we would throw lines into the evening airs: 'Meantime
we shall express our darker purpose.' Or: 'Sure, her offence
must be of such unnatural degree that monsters it.' Or: 'You
nimble lightnings, dart your blinding flames!' Or: 'Blow,
winds, and crack your cheeks! rage! blow! You cataracts and
hurricanoes.' After which, I would to my house and he to
his to sup our own suppers and dream the separate parts
of our dream.

"In those days," Linus Lancaster my dead husband said
to me, "Louisville was still something worth the shooting,
and a man of caliber could make himself a man of property if he had a way with the world and his hands around
the throat of a salable notion, and that was me. That was
me! I could sing like one of God's own angels, could strut
the stage and turn a line, and there wasn't a man in
Kentucky could charm a creature like I could. Once, when
I was just down to Louisville and getting started, I had had
to take Bennett Marsden by the scrawny arm and throw
him out the door because he had come between me and
some of the flora arrived to us by boat from Baton Rouge.
This was at auction, and when I saw her I had to have her,
and I had had her and now she was in my home. Bennett
Marsden had thought to have her, but it was I who had
offered up the best pile of coin. Some several years had
scrawled on past since that affair, and the business had been
forgotten. Bennett Marsden had found himself one or two

fine ones I wouldn't have argued against tasting, but the fever took them. It never touched mine.

"'The World,' I would tell my lady creature of an evening. 'The World, yes, that's a dandy name for a theater,' she would say. One night, when the theater was finished, we said this back and forth as I had at my own bottle then at her, and I went out with my paintbrush in the moonlight and the next morning all the city walked by my sign. When Bennett Marsden came he said nothing, but clapped me on the shoulder and acknowledged that my paintwork was fine.

"We draped the World in gold and purple and spread out word that we would have us a performance after a fortnight," my dead husband, Linus Lancaster, went on. "We beat the bushes and banged the drum and sold every bench place in the house. We were to play a shortened version of *Lear* and I was to be Lear and Bennett Marsden my good Gloucester. There were some boys for the other parts and two fine fat ladies Bennett Marsden had found for us to play the three daughters. We rehearsed each night then drank, and after we had drunk I would sit one or both those fine fat ladies across my knees. Bennett Marsden would chuckle when I did this then fill my glass full. They told me there was enough of me for both of them, and as you well know, Wife, this was true. Sometimes when I had them on my knees I would sing. All I had to do was open my mouth and they would all shut theirs. This was also true. Everything I say is true. Many was the time after the rehearsals and this knee-bending with the ladies that

Bennett Marsden had his boys or mine carry me home. At home I knee-bended with my own fair creature maiden then slept as something come to the end of its good long labors. Normal times I slept a deep and happy blank, but one night I had the purest vision of a field filled with pigs and me the happiest man alive in the middle of it. You know of that dream.

"We opened to a house as full as the World could hold. One of the boys played a flute and the other a drum. Come time for it and they put their hands together and you couldn't have heard a word. I stepped out onto the stage for a speech with Gloucester and I took in my breath and let it roar. I said my speech and pulled my wig hair and wept a tear, but when I had finished the house wasn't weeping. I said 'fog, fen, and bash' with every ounce I had but none stirred. Nor did Gloucester stir, so I said some of my speech again. Him as Gloucester came over to me and whispered up at my ear: 'We're playing *Coriolanus,* act four.'

"'We're playing shortened *Lear,*' I said. 'Enough with your jokes now.'

"'I am King Lear,' I said aloud. I stepped around the stage. I gave the fresh planks some whacks with my foot. I said some of my lines from farther along.

"'Come, leave your tears; a brief farewell: the beast with many heads butts me away . . .' he said, in a stage whisper, plenty loud enough for the hall to hear.

"The room laughed with it. Some of them held up their programs. I had never seen these programs. They must have been passed out while I was at my preparations. *Coriolanus at the World,* they read.

"I stepped to the side and as I did, the boy who had been beating the drum and the two fine fat ladies Bennett Marsden had found for us stepped onstage, and after he had made a speech to the crowd about lightness and levity and my good nature to launch off the World's first show with such a *flourish,* he started in on *Coriolanus* and the others played it right along with him. I had on my Lear wig and my Lear crown and all my Lear lines in my head. I saw straightaway the trick he had played me, understood the payment he had given me for my World. I left out the back door. Walked the alleys home. On the way I passed a creature hauling its master in a little wagon. The master was awake and singing a courting song, the creature had a purple hat on its head.

"That night I dreamed my own creatures hauled me out of Louisville with bits in their mouths. That I sat in the driver's seat and they stood in for the horses. That I whipped them till the froth flew, till they howled against the metal, till we all fell over dead."

"You sure fell," I said when he had at last stopped. "Right over onto your face in the kitchen light."

He nodded.

"Anyways, I already heard all about the way of the World and liked the first telling better; it came with a dance," I said.

He gave out a smaller smile this time and adjusted the pig sticker in his neck and nodded again.

"You can see why we broke off our association, me and Bennett Marsden."

"You mean I can see why you broke it off. Why maybe you left him holding the bills. Left him to carry all the load."

He smiled.

"Why did you wait so long?" he asked me before he left.

"I don't know," I said.

The next morning I stood at the kitchen door and waved the Draper Man back off down the lane.

"I'll call to see your husband, who owes me money from our business together, before the fortnight, Mrs. Lancaster," he called. "I'll add that it will be a pleasure to see you again too."

"Good journey, Mr. Bennett Marsden," I called back.

Before he had broken out of sight I had stepped back into the kitchen again.

8.

IT WAS LUCIOUS WILSON thought I might be quick with a piece of chalk and one day asked me was I interested in tending the school he had it in mind to set up. He had people in his employ, and those people had children and he had his own, and the only school nearby was farther away than he liked to send them. He had seen me gobbling at the books on his shelves and had watched me help his children make their numbers and letters and had a feeling it would work out right. He had hired a teacher from Marion to come out by autumntime and had a shed at the edge of one of the fields that would make a fine school by then, but if I was willing to work in rough conditions I could get it going now. He would see to the slates and primers and make sure I had what I needed.

He put this to me while I was scraping spilled oatmeal off the wall in his front hall. He had his hands kind of slipped into the pockets of his purple vest as he spoke. This was still in my early days in his employ. They hadn't started in to call me Scary. He had seen the fresh blood on my ankle but hadn't blinked. I was still what you could call young then and had been some time away by then from Charlotte County, and some of the freshness of strong young arms and strong young legs had likely bubbled up into my head and made me think some of the furniture had floated back into its right place, and I set down my scraper and looked up at Lucious Wilson and told him, yes.

"Good," he said and went away with a whistle, and I picked my scraper back up and went to work on the oatmeal, but a week later I found myself wearing a snug black dress and neat black shoes and standing at the front of the room. There were six or eight of them, depending on the day and the farming weather, that Lucious Wilson had directed into my charge. They sat on benches with a slate each in their laps, and I had a chair in the corner I could move to if I needed it and there were windows to look out of and fine black fields all around. I had asked Lucious Wilson for a map of the country and some paper to draw big letters and numbers on and with them had decorated my abode. The pride of the whole thing was the chalkboard. It had been brought up by wagon from Indianapolis. Lucious Wilson said the shed might still be rough, but it would have a chalkboard. I wrote my name on that board the first day. I wrote, "Miss Sue."

She's dreaming, you will have said to yourself by now. She's old and life-kicked and set to dreaming about things that never happened. Ginny Lancaster of Charlotte County, Kentucky, or Scary Sue the oatmeal scrubber, a schoolteacher.

And yet there I stood those mornings in my black dress. There I was.

There wasn't much to the first day or two. I had Lucious Wilson's little ones and another little one and then a fistful that were all but grown. Not a body in the room knew its letters to speak of, so we started there. My trick about it was to pretend I was in that old schoolroom of mine, that room where I had written my story and been called to the front of the class. I could even bring up the pine smell of that place, and it wasn't a thing to imagine that my old teacher was standing just behind me with a lit-tle smile, whispering at me about what to say. We did let-ters and took a peek at numbers and sang songs, and another few of those days mooed and grazed their way by. Lucious Wilson liked to come in at the end of a morning and stand in the doorway. Once he came a nob early, and I had him step up to the front of the room and give us a song. He couldn't sing worth shooting, but there was fun in it and we all clapped.

"This is fine, Sue," he said afterward. "Just fine."

The trouble came up on the second week. It sat in the lap of one of the bigger ones, who one morning looked me up and looked me down, then said, "You ain't our teacher. You ain't any teacher at all."

I came over to see if she was having trouble with the letters I had set them to practice. It was when I got up close and saw her in her profile, her profile with its little bit of a snarl to it, that I started to smell the trouble that had snuck its way into the room through the chinks in the shed wall while I had stood there in my teacher dress and teacher shoes, while I stood there with my chalk and letters and chair in the corner to sit on. I smelled the trouble, but still I looked down at what she had marked on her slate. She tried to hide it away from me but I saw it before she did. It was a pig dressed as a teacher. Thick of middle and long of snout. A pig to switch off to market. To stick and hang. To have its hairs scalded off. To butcher into its portions of truth. It was easy to see even at a quick glance that she had some talent with an image, that the rendering was fair. I went back and stood in front of them for a minute. Only I wasn't in my teacher's dress and my teacher's shoes any longer, and my old teacher had left me to myself and I could feel the weight of Zinnia's pig-slop hat on my head.

"She's crying," one of them said.

I hadn't known it. But I was.

The shed had a little door to its back, behind the chalkboard. I stood there and cried a stretch longer then stepped through it. I went around the side of the shed and bent and picked hard at my ankle, then stood and smacked my face into its wall.

She was nice to me afterward, the one who had drawn the pig on her slate. She grew all the way up and got married to a blacksmith who put her into nice dresses and got her a nice carriage to drive around. I used to see her at the church. She died some time ago. Not of anything special.

It wasn't any length of time after I had left off playing schoolteacher and gone back to the scrub brushes and oatmeal that my employer Lucious Wilson called on me to keep him some company. He was drifting through his days and wanted someone to latch an anchor to them, is what he told me. He also told me I had a glow on me that he admired the sheen of. His children favored me. They had cried when I stopped being their teacher. They were always hollering for more of my stories. My stories that weren't about black bark or wet dough. Just those good old ones about falling down wells and burning boots and girls with long golden hair. He wanted to know was I committed elsewhere. Did I have any company I was keeping or hoping to keep? Was anyone waiting on me wherever it was I had come up from? He knew the answer to this but asked it anyway. He was young then. He bowed a little with his head when he talked and didn't look at me too long in the eyes.

He made me this little speech and question as we walked out in the west flatlands where they kept the cattle back then. Everywhere you looked there were beasts working the green. A young bull came up and snuffled Lucious Wilson's fingers. Turkey buzzards lolled circles above the north woods. There was sun on it all. A good sun. Lord of days, a glow to me, the pig lady from Charlotte County that the water doesn't want, I thought.

I kept a kind of company with Lucious Wilson for a time then. For a time, after it was dark and his children were asleep and it was only me and the drafts in the halls,

I would trip along to my employer's room and take off my bonnet and, at his bidding, crawl into his bed. Night after night and time after time I would trip up the stair and down the corridor and tap on his door. There was things I thought as I made that passage, and times the trouble that had found me out in that school shed found me out in that passage, and it took me to turn around midway and run back to my own room and hide under the covers and scratch at my ankle with a paring knife. Times as I walked that my legs grew longer and my feet heavier and my chest as big as a barrel and my head the size of a salt block. My hands would swing like slabs of hard stone and I would walk down that corridor, ahead and alongside of myself with a different door in mind. Here I am a-comin', girls, I thought. I might even have said it aloud. Linus Lancaster said it once in Kentucky as he passed my shut door and went toward the other. So I might have said it too.

One night when I had only made it half the way and was back in my bed and under the covers, Lucious Wilson knocked on my door. He had followed me, he said. He had heard me coming and had had his heart quickened and had had to come after me when I had turned around. He lit the candle and sat down on my bed and pulled the covers down off of my face.

"I'll take that knife you got under there too," he said.

I gave it to him. He was a good man. He had that kindness in his eyes and hands and was as soft as a box of baby chicks in his bedroom ways. Lucious Wilson set the knife aside and laid himself down gentle next to me and we both lay there and looked up at the ceiling with our arms crossed over our chests and he said we were lying there like a king and queen of olden days, and I asked him if the olden days were better than the days we had, and he said who could know such a thing?

"I would have rescued you up out of whatever situation it was, Sue," he said. "I would have brought my rifle and stiffed my jaw and marched into whatever it was and got you out," he said.

We used a kind of lavender on his shirt linens. I could smell that when he talked to me. You could smell it drifting through that whole house of his. That's what heaven in the hereafter smells like, I thought, as he laid there next to me and talked.

"Yes, I expect you would have tried, I can see that," I said. "Only there was no way to know where I was. No road through the woods to find me. Only breadcrumbs to lay on the ground and birds weighting down all the branches above."

He was quiet after I'd said this and even quieter after what I said next. "And if you had found me, it might not have been me you chose to help."

The next day in the forenoon he asked me to clasp hands in the parlor with him and pray. Then he asked me to be his wife. Those and their cousins, said right and by the right body, are kind words. I don't know any kinder. And I told my employer Lucious Wilson that. Then I told him no. I could not stand by him as he had asked. I told him I had been down in hell and that hell was not a place

you left no matter how far you hauled your bones away
from it. It had found me in his school shed and it had found
me in the passage of his house and it would find me again.
I was not fit to be his or anyone else's wife, I told him. I
looked him all the time in the eye as I said this. Then I went
to pack my bag. Lucious Wilson came and stood in the
doorway a long while watching me. He lit his pipe and
breathed of it and the smoke came out into the room.

If I could have gathered myself up and turned into
smoke then I would have. I would have joined my smoke
to his and drifted on out the window and stuck for a while
to the floors Lucious Wilson walked on and to the walls
where he leaned his hands. There is a fragrance to a good
pipe smoke I have always been partial to.

There is a pipe here in this very room I will sometimes
pull out and take a chew on. I do not light my pipe. I do
not chuck it full of tobacco. I think of the smoke Lucious
Wilson put out into the room, even all those years ago now,
and how I stood there and worked over my few things and
my bag. Some of the times as I chew on my pipe I bite
down hard and play it that I did gather myself up that day
and did turn to smoke, and that as I drifted he breathed me
in then blew me out fresh into his arms. He carried me
away then down the hall and out of this world to another
where you can put all that you've hurt and all that's hurt
you behind like an old cracked honey jar. I expect I was
already dreaming some of that as I stood there at my bed.
Where would that place be and who would have arms
strong enough to carry you there? I expect I thought.

He spoke his soft, good things to me one more time, and one more time I told him no. Then he knocked out his pipe, nodded, and said, "All right now, Sue, I'll not trouble you longer," and told me to put my things back on the shelf.

This morning there was a light-skinned colored man come riding down the road that cuts through the middle of Lucious Wilson's lands and leads right up past the front porch of this little house. He had on a gray hat and gray suit, and his horse wasn't wanting for being combed and curried. Just like a prince on the palace grounds he looked. You couldn't have told he was colored but I could see it, in the eyebrows, in the handsome oils of his hair. I was out airing my carcass in the springtime breezes, and when he passed on by me he nodded and lifted his hat and I nodded back, and I said to myself, "Colored man, go safe."

I did say this.

I don't ask that you believe me or that you don't.

A body believes what it will and wants to. There is no rule to any of it. No recipe.

When I was coming up north out of my four-square kingdom, I feared the day and walked the dark, but when I saw folks I fluttered toward them like I was a moth and they were some fine snack of light. Still, there wasn't any wayfarer would have me long enough to take a good look. What was there to have? Some rags and flaps of skin with curly horns sprouting out of its head? Scary Sue come running up out of Charlotte County. Out of Paradise with its weathers fair.

I come upon a child one of those evenings I was walking. I crossed a creek and had froth on my rags and come on that pretty child playing with a spoon and biscuit and set it to screaming. Not a night later a man with a knife and a coonskin on his head crawled up on me in the dark, but when I stood into the moonlight and he saw what he was stalking he crawled away again.

On the banks of the Ohio River I parlayed in the moonlight with a ferryman who looked me up and looked me down and said he needed no coin from me because I had already paid. I had the black bark in my pocket, he said, and the black bark in my pocket meant *pass*. It didn't matter where I went, where I thought I could go. I could change my apron anytime I wanted to and it would still be there waiting in my pocket. He knew. He had two sisters who came up as he was talking and took me back to where they did their washing and scrubbed me down like I was just some old clothes to fret on the board. One of them had a frock to spare, and she dropped it over my head when they were done. The other had a pair of boots to put on my feet, and she put them there. Neither a one of them spoke a word as they did this.

The ferryman had me climb up on his boat directly they were finished with me. After we had crossed and I had set my foot on hard dirt, he told me, "Go safe now, Mother," and I turned and saw it was Alcofibras sitting there, his hands covered in eyes and raised up off the oars into the mist.

"Where have you taken me, Alcofibras?" I asked him.

"Go on now, Mother," he said.

I walked for another week, and when I got back to my father's house I found him and my mother gone and their house with my corner in it burned to the ground. I'd worn my rotten boots out getting there and went barefoot over to Evansville. There was talk everywhere about war. Young men with drink in them bunched up in lines and marched along the thoroughfare. There was considerable discharging of rifles. I told it when they asked that I had walked up out of fire. Not out of Charlotte County, Kentucky. Not out of Paradise and murder.

9.

THAT DAY WE SAW OFF Bennett Marsden I went back into the kitchen like I've already said. I had on my dress and had my clean hands, and because I thought what we had been cooking up for Bennett Marsden was still sitting on the stove, I stood up straight when I got to the table and I told Zinnia to sit. I told her to sit, and she looked at me like there was lightning and thunder to come, but she sat. Then I told Cleome to walk down the hall to Linus Lancaster's room and fetch a wallet out of a drawer she would find half hidden in the chifforobe. Cleome said she would not walk into Linus Lancaster's room, and who was I to be handing out orders. I told her again. Zinnia nodded. Cleome went and fetched it. When she got it to the table I took it from her, told her to sit, and opened it up past its few notions to a portrait in a leather frame. That was a photographic portrait of a lady wearing a hat.

"Linus Lancaster, my late husband who is gone now to his pigs and glory, liked to show us this," I said. I showed it up to Cleome then to Zinnia. "He liked to hold this up to us like I'm holding this up to you now, and he liked to say everything he'd ever loved in this world and everything he'd ever hoped to bring to his piece of paradise was in this frame. This was usually after his singing nights. When he had been at the jug. Do you remember this?"

"All right," said Zinnia. She said this without moving her lips, without moving her eyes, which had lingered only a moment on the portrait, from mine. Cleome said nothing.

"All right," I said, then pulled the first piece of tin up out of the frame and revealed the second behind it and held it up in its turn. Cleome and Zinnia looked at each other then at me.

"I found this second one just this winter," I said.

Neither one of them said a word. Only looked at me. There was a cold breeze at my ankles. It tickled at the bruises there. Rose up hackles on my neck.

"I am sorry," I said. "I just wish to say that to you both now. That is what I wish to say."

"Sorry about what?" said Cleome.

Zinnia reached into her apron, pulled the pig sticker out, and, holding it lengthwise, looked at it close.

"If he was sitting here with us, I would stand and put this right back into his neck," she said.

"It would slide easy into that neck," she said.

"Sloooosh now, Mother," she said.

Cleome gave out a little laugh. There was a tear on her face. One silver drop. We all three of us watched it move down her cheek, around the mole, down her neck. There was a first fly buzzing by the door. It spoke of insects hatching everywhere. Things hidden inching up. Once upon a time the three of us had played a game to see who could spot the first wild crocus, the first mosquito, the first open bud. I almost said "First fly!" even knowing that whatever we had been cooking up for Bennett Marsden, the Draper Man, had gone cold and crumpled like heavy old biscuits to put holes through the floor.

Cleome put a hand on her stomach and looked at me.

"Sorry about what, Mother?" she whispered. "What do you have to be sorry for?"

They fed me awhile then took me back out to the shed.

There was a reverend at the little church here awhile back who taught it that in your beginnings are your endings, and that when you hit your endings you have just begun. He taught it every Sunday like that, twisting it up with David and Moses and Josiah and every one of the apostles, and you should have seen them all scratching their heads and nodding and shaking the reverend's hand when he was done. Now one of those Sundays while he was telling it about Mary and leaving off her one sorry life to get started on her blessed other, my head lolled, and as he discussed this I chased my way into thinking about my father and how he was in the early days before the war had ravished off his foot. Our little place in Indiana was a sunny place in those days, and my father liked to pick me up and give me a twirl. He had been in battles before and had his marks to prove it, but they hadn't yet found a way to take away his foot from him, and he liked to tell stories about his wars and the wide world in which he had fought them.

"You think the world is this big," my father would say and hold his hands one across from the other. "But it's really this big," he would say and stretch his hands as far as he could apart. "It's that big and then some and on across the oceans until you get back to where you set off. We could hitch up that wagon and roll it until the horses died of old age in their harnesses and we wouldn't have even gotten started. I've seen ladies taking their tea in ships in harbors it would take a week to sail across and boys racing up trees they said were a thousand years old. Someday we're going to ride it on out of here and plant our flag in the Kansas Territories or the Oregon country or sail right off to China. They make maps so we think we can understand the size of it but we can't."

My father came into my school where I sat in the front row and wasn't yet a wife to my mother's second cousin or an oatmeal scrubber or a pretend teacher or anything at all, and he made a speech about the world to us. The Lord had given us eyes to see with and feet to get us to where it could all be seen, he said. It was up to us to go out and see, to go out and consider. That was our work. We ought to strap up our shoes and set to it. The worst we could do was fail. And all fail meant was we had grit enough to try. We all clapped when he had finished and he gave a bow.

Then my father put on his belt and went off to a battle and took a tomahawk or some such in his foot, and they cut that foot off of him and threw it out into the field for the crows.

"I could see them out there after it from my sickbed," he said. "It wasn't even the best of them made off with the biggest part."

Those last days in the shed my father's foot came down out of those crows' stomachs and reconstituted itself and kept me company. Does a foot shorn of its leg sit or stand? I put that query to it, but it didn't answer. There was more ankle and leg to it than I would have thought. Once or twice it fell over on its side. Its heel was cracked. You could have planted fine rows of seeds in those cracks. Could have watered them and tended them and had a springtime show. I thought this. And I said it aloud. Or thought I did.

Does your father's lost foot need talking to? Does it require attention? Does it need to be fed? Do you rock your father's lost foot in your arms. Do you sing it a lullaby? Do you tie it to a tree and take your whip to it? Is your father's lost foot the beginning or the end?

I've had nights lately when it came to me that I had never left that shed. That everything up to that point and everything after it happened in there.

Is happening in there.

Is that my beginning or my ending?

I'll burn this stack of sheets when I'm done.

As it came to pass they did not put the pig sticker that had been in Linus Lancaster's neck into my own. This had been the subject of debate and considerable discussion in light of Bennett Marsden's promised return. I know this because they both of them walked into the shed where I lay shackled in my declivity more than once and then walked back out again. Zinnia came always with the pig sticker. On some occasions she was preceded by Cleome and others she was followed by her. One time she walked all the way up to me and turned me over and put the point of it at the nape under my hair. Then she pulled it back up and walked away and left me lying facedown. Cleome was quiet each time. They both only talked when they were walking away. I could not hear what they said. I knew it was Cleome arguing mercy and Zinnia mercy's opposite. It had always been this way. Cleome soft. Zinnia hard.

Then they left. They took their leave one bright morning in what I later pieced out was early June. I had been sleeping and then I was awake and saw Zinnia standing out by the well. Cleome was some yards ahead, a sack on her back, big as her front. My old traveling hat with its pink ribbon on her head.

Zinnia said, "Peace on you now, Mother Ginny. We're done." As she said this she held up a key. I knew what key that was. She held it up then dropped it down into the well.

"You hear a splash?" Cleome called.

Zinnia didn't answer her. She looked in at me. I thought she nodded. Nodded with her eyes at me. I'd had nor food nor water for three days. There was none left near me. The key to my shackle was dropped down Linus Lancaster's well. Cleome had moved out of sight into her tomorrow. Still Zinnia stood. She looked in the direction Cleome had gone, then she looked back at me. Her lips were moving. A song came over to me. It was a song we'd sung. All three of us together. Picking daisies on hell's front porch in the long ago.

All that last day I looked out through the door. I looked through it all that night, and the night was rich in moon and I could see the well. I'll come swimming down you, I thought. I will swim the wide dark ways of the earth. I will dive down and swim out into your corridors of water and stone. I will shiver my soul through your rooms draped in midnight fruit and flower and deliver myself dripping unto the fire and take my place at Linus Lancaster's side. I will stand beside him as that wet sizzles off me, and if they sing in hell I will stand next to my husband and sing, and maybe in hell where they have different ways my small voice will drown his big voice out.

I will do this, I thought. They have thrown my death down into the well and I will follow it. I followed it. The gibbous moon draped itself down over my world, lit my way. There was no splash when I hit water.

It was good into the forenoon of that last morning when I saw what I had not seen all that day and night for following my death: a piece of purple thread strung taut from the beam behind me and out through the motes aswirl in the shed light to the lip of the well and over into that hole. I knew I was dreaming it, but my hand went out and took it and pulled and, dreaming, hauled it hand over hand until the key had come out of its wet and its dark. I dreamed it came down on the yard dirt with a thump of dust and that I pulled it through the shed dirt and into my hand. My dream played dreaming tricks with me and at first wouldn't let the key into the lock of my shackle. My eyes looked at my hands and my hands at the lock and the key would not enter and after it had entered would not turn. Then it did. I dreamed my way up out of my filth and my shed and walked bloody-ankled to the edge of the well and saw the dream of my face down below amid the dark water. Zinnia or Cleome or both had drunk of that water before they departed and they had left the bucket half-filled on the far side where I had not seen it from the shed. I woke from my dream with that bucket at my lips. I woke and ran.

10.

I SLEPT EASY in that cold frame I came to rest in behind Lucious Wilson's outhouse easier than I slept in any bed before or after, in company or alone. The dirt to it was soft, and as I lay there the nights I did I sunk enough to put me back into my hole in that shed in Kentucky. I dug out that hole with my fingers. They had gotten me used to putting myself down into the dirt during the daytime, and when they put me away at night I got to favoring the idea of a shallow hole to make my bed in. All those weeks and months previous, in Evansville and Indianapolis, I had been thinking about that hole. About where I had been dead and waiting for the pig sticker to put the final word to it. I found it again in that cold frame behind the outhouse.

Before she passed I told the old woman who found me and took me to Lucious Wilson about that. About that and about my husband's piece of paradise and about my breakfasts with him. I told her about the pigs running wild and my hugging the oak tree and the shackle and watching Alcofibras at his turn. That old woman liked to sip fresh mint tea to settle her before sleeping, and as I talked she sat there and sipped it. Every now and again she would pick a mint leaf off her tongue. I told her about taking the strop to Zinnia and about taking the strop to Cleome. I told her I had not raised my voice against my husband when he was at Alcofibras. I told her I had tempted Linus Lancaster into taking me down to Kentucky to live in his fine house with him. That I had sat in his big lap and tickled his ear with a piece of timothy.

"Well, well, Sue," she said. "The Lord has his ways and meanings for us all."

"The water moved away from me. It wouldn't have me," I said.

"I know it. I know it."

She had crop-colored eyes and a nice way of speaking. She died two days later when a horse kicked her in the head.

If it hadn't, I could have told her that I had not stopped taking the strop to Cleome even after I saw her sick in the mornings nor when Zinnia told me why and begged me to give her Cleome's and her own lickings both. Or that it was ten days and nights of stroppings and visits down the hall from the time I found that second photographic portrait in my husband's drawer in the chifforobe, on the back of which had been written, in my husband's own hand, "dearly departed and my two daughters," to the night I pulled the pig sticker out of the moon-slathered sow Linus Lancaster had lately slaughtered and hung up by the barn and came up behind him as he sat to a late whiskey, singing with that voice of his, and gristled every speck of it into his neck.

I cannot account for that delay. There was a fury in me. It is there still.

A time as I was coming up north through the twilight, heading for the river with its ferryman, a rider with black teeth leaned down off his horse and asked me what I was running from.

"You're looking at it," I said.

I also cannot give a reason why I did not finish the second part of the chore I'd set myself that evening and apply that pig sticker to myself. Or why, having left it sit there in Linus Lancaster, I didn't pack up my bag and run. I knew it wasn't kisses I had coming.

You'd have thought I enjoyed that jaunt there in the shed. Was gobbling up my just desserts. Taking what was mine and earned. Giving it a hiss and a grin. Letting my fury out into the young days of Kentucky to turn a step and a bow with theirs.

Once in my deepest early days a boy got lost and fell into a pond, and when they found him he was just a blue coat and red pants floating facedown under ten inches of ice. My father went out with his axe to help get him out. All the men had axes and they made a kind of clock on the ice and took turns letting their axes fall. The axes fell one after the other around the clock, and pieces of ice flew up into the air and off to the sides and caught the sunlight coming down into the crater they were making. I was five. The boy had been my playmate. It looked like they were pulling him out of the eye of a jewel. When they had him out and were wrapping him on the bank, I walked over to the jewel crackling around the black water and just dropped myself in. It was my father who pulled me out. When he had me home and dry and hugged, he whipped me until I saw the same stars I'd seen around that jewel in the pond, and then he whipped me some more because when he asked me if I'd had enough licking, I started to smile.

Comes a day when everything you thought you had put behind you sets up its tent in the middle of what you were still hoping you could call tomorrow and yells out, "Right this way."

Well, here I come.

CANDLE STORY

(WHERE THEY WENT)
1911 / 1861

But they'll nor pinch,
Fright me with urchin-shows, pitch me i' the mire,
Nor lead me, like a firebrand, in the dark

I WAS EIGHTEEN YEARS OLD in 1861. What I walked away from one late spring morning in Kentucky I vowed never to walk toward again. The long years went by and I kept my vow. Then this notion came upon me. It put a hand on my shoulder as I sat to my Sunday prayer. It put a hand on my shoulder and squeezed.

I carried it here. All the days and nights it took to make the journey. When I was eighteen and my sister was sixteen and we walked away together. Held hands and walked, the two of us, away across the stone bridge. There was a Klaxon as that hand squeezed my shoulder.

It must have been just outside the church. I started and sat up straight, caught Eunice Fairbanks's eye and we both gave a laugh. That laugh covered up the feeling of that other thing well enough that it wasn't until I was on my way out of the church that I thought of it again. The Reverend Washington was standing out on the street shaking hands, sending off his blessings. I told Prosper, my nephew, to wait and asked the Reverend if I could have a moment. We stood away from the traffic, leaned in close to each other against the noise. I told him it was the old days come to visit. He asked me if they wanted anything in particular. I told him that they did, that I had felt a call.

"Stay here with us, Granny," he said. "You fought all the fight of this world. Stay right here. Let others fight now. Take your rest."

The Reverend Washington is a fine young man. He tends to the poor and holds the hands of the sick. Once I saw him lift a car off a little white boy who had been thrown under it. They give trouble to some of the colored churches but not to ours. Prosper has been right to seek his counsel a number of times. I thanked him. He was born long after the old days. I asked him if he would pray a moment with me.

I went when Cleome had fallen deep into her sleep in the corner we had taken for ourselves in the barn. I saw one of the old sows, easing an itch on the oak tree, as I made my way and held my hand up to my head against the bats swooping all around. The candle I had brought did nothing in the bright moonlight. When I reached the shed, I set it on a ledge then went and looked at her. I could see fresh blood, black in the candlelight, seeping around her ankle where the iron cut. She was asleep.

I worked quietly, hooking the far end of the thread to the same bracket that held her chain, weaving the line up over two of the shiny roof beams. Then I took it over the nail stopper in the door and out into the moonlight. The sow was done and had flopped down into a pile by the tree. There were others of her kind around, you could hear them snoring off in the dark. I don't know when they had stopped fearing bears and wolves, maybe they had all gotten too big to care about things with teeth, and certainly we never troubled them anymore. I took the thread three strong loops around the key as I stood next to the well and left it sitting on the edge. Then I walked my way backward all the way to the bracket, pulling on the line as I went to make sure it was strong. She stirred as I walked by so I had to kick her, make her think I was there for other reasons. It wasn't hard to pretend. It was not pretend. She barely gave a murmur, though I had kicked her in the neck. I took my candle down off the ledge.

"I'll see you again in the morning, Mother Ginny," I said.

Cleome was sitting up when I got back.

"Couldn't sleep?" she asked.

I nodded. I had her lie back down on the hay and I rubbed her legs. Presently, she was giving out her soft little snores. Sunlight came to wake us all soon enough.

I knew just where it was. After my talk with the Reverend Washington outside of the church, I went and stood in front of the drawer I'd set it in years before. Hidden behind a hairbrush and a pincushion. A bundle of needles. A square of orange cloth.

I am old but I am not yet tired, and I have gotten to live on all these years with Prosper in this place, I thought. I have risen from deep waters and I have kept on, I thought. Fifty years have gone by. I have my vow, I have my life, I thought.

I packed my travel bag, put on my travel hat, and walked out the door. Prosper caught up with me when I got to Michigan Avenue, said to find me he had just followed the trail of everyone I'd walked by like I was some kind of a ghost. I told Prosper that people could think what they wanted and that ghost or not, I was bound on business for Kentucky. Prosper looked at me, saw I meant it, took my bag, and said that if Kentucky was *our* destination we had best take the train. I asked him about his work at the stone yard. He said his work could wait: he had seen the look in my eye.

The train took us all of a rattle down to Louisville, Louisville of my first dreams. I did not shudder when we stepped off the platform. I did not shudder when our search for a wagon took us near where I had lived as a small girl. For years when the bad part of the past times have come to me, I have nodded my head, set my jaw, and looked them in the eye until they have left again. I did no different now that I had come to them. The wagon Prosper

rented for us had a pallet in the back where I could recline.
Part of the time as we rolled toward Charlotte County I lay
on my back with my head on my traveling bag and looked
up at the sky. Every now and then I would lift up and call
out some direction to Prosper, but otherwise I just lay
there. I was on my back, like a dead thing, when we rolled
over the stone bridge.

"We're here now, Aunt Zinnia, wherever that here is,"
Prosper said.

"Paradise," I said, sitting up, preparing to crack the yolk
of my eyes over that world once more. "Paradise is what
we called it."

The barn and house and oak tree were gone. But the
well was still there. And the shed. I climbed into the front
of the wagon and Prosper went to knock on the door of
the house that stood now where the barn had been. I kept
my eyes on the well. There was no door on the front of
the shed. A couple came out of the house with Prosper, like
us but darker-skinned.

"How do?" said the man.

"You will have to forgive me," I said as they came over.
"Now that I am here I see that I will not be able to get
down."

"Aunt Z?" said Prosper.

"You want some cool tea, honey?" said the woman.

But I did not answer them; how could I answer them?
For there I was again, standing over what lay shackled unto
its misery in that shed. And there I sat, myself, with the
shackle on my arm and a rat at my foot. And there leaned

Cleome, her back wet from fresh whipping, the rain dripping onto her head through the holes in the roof. And there stood Alcofibras, the chain wrapped around his neck, refusing to sit even though he was kept there for two days. That shed where I had kicked and been kicked. I sat on the wagon and I sat inside of that shed but never moved. The thing at my feet moved. I kicked it. We'll speak on this someday, I thought.

Still and all, I came to myself and made some apology then learned that the couple had indeed heard of a Ginestra Lancaster, that not two months before a white man down from Indiana had knocked on their door to ask if she had any people over this way. She was getting on in her years, was Ginestra Lancaster, and this man's and her employer, Lucious Wilson, had sent him from Clinton County to see if he could give any shake to the family tree. The couple had never heard of any Lancasters and had had the farm in their family more than forty years. The man had left them with five dollars for their trouble.

"Clinton County, Indiana?" I said, although I had heard it well enough.

The woman nodded. I could see she really did want to give me a glass of her tea. I drank it sitting in the wagon, knowing the coolness to it had come up out of the well. The man said a word or two about the luck we'd had on our errand in coming to them so soon after the white man from Indiana, and the woman said that luck had nothing to do with it or anything else in the Lord's domain.

"Aren't I right, honey?" she said to me.

She was, but I didn't answer. I was back in the shed. Only this time it was all of us in there at the same time. Rats and pigs and people. As we rode away I did not tell Prosper that he had been here before too, that he had floated in his first waters on this farm, that although his tiny feet had never touched its rocks and soils, he had been with us, both in the shed and out of it, when I and his mother had taken hands together and walked away.

She said it was like taking rocks out of her pockets and dropping them to the ground. Every day she would unload the rocks, one by one, and every morning, when she woke, they would be there again. We walked and the rocks fell from her hands. I wanted to know if it felt a little lighter at the start of each new day and she said it didn't, but that the rocks were dropping all the same. We kept to the side lanes, went to the ditches when we heard horses, as Horace and Ulysses had told us we must when we left. The closer we got to Louisville the more there were men with whips and guns. Neither one of us had left the farm since we had arrived, but we made our way just the same. We had corn pone and salt pork to eat and water from the streams. We had a Bible, from our mother, which we had kept hidden away for years to read aloud to each other. We could both of us read; our mother had seen to that before her owner and ours had beaten her to death. I carried everything. I did not speak of purple thread. Cleome had the child and her rocks and her time was near.

When we got to Louisville we found Horace and Ulysses living in a basement, doing night work at the docks. Cleome said she couldn't live in any basement. Horace and Ulysses were scared to have someone in her condition on their hands, and fretted considerably at first. Still, we waited one week with them in their hole.

As we waited, we talked and read the Bible and told each other stories about how we thought it would be up north. Horace and Ulysses said there was a war coming, that the whole world would be swept away, that we would all be struck down, but we hardly heard them. Our ears were either still back in Paradise or on up the road, but not there. Cleome sat quiet for long stretches. She had a piece of sewing work she would worry at while she sat. She had always been quick with her fingers, but now they were swollen. I rubbed her hands and her feet.

She never complained, just said she wanted to get walking and dropping her rocks out of her pockets again. There were times, as I rubbed and her head lolled, and I looked at her belly, that I would give a shiver and hear heavy feet coming down the corridor, but that would pass.

I only went out once, to fetch a woman who had known my mother to look to Cleome. That woman worked in a house next to the one my mother had died in, that I had first been set to work in, that I had taken my first beatings in. After I had gotten her to agree to come, I stood for a while outside that house. It was an ugly thing with cracked boards and a bad roof. A hickory tree stood in front. It had gotten taller over the years. Cleome and I had climbed it one time and waved at our mother, who was sitting at her work by the fire. My mother's name was Flora Keckley. She was soft with us. She worked every day of her life. He would come home in the evening, drunk or not. Some nights he brought presents, others his fists. I knew I shouldn't be standing out on the street in broad daylight, but it took me some while to pull myself away from that ugly house with its hickory tree.

The woman came to our hole that night and said she didn't like the look of Cleome at all. She said the child was carrying wrong and would have to be turned. She worked at this some time then gave up with a shrug.

"You need to stay still," the woman said.

"She can't," I said.

She gave us two packets of herbs and made Cleome eat a paste she had ground up. Two days later we rode five miles out of town buried under cotton bales.

Cleome suffered a great deal during the ride, but she kept talking about letting those rocks drop away. The world had eaten all the sweetness out of her, but there she was lying under the bales, her face next to mine, smiling. The first thing we did when we were out of that cart and hidden in some bushes was pray. We had thirty miles to walk and only darkness to do our walking in.

"The Bible is a cheer when there is darkness about."

Cleome said this and stood when night had fallen. We held hands, pointed our way forward, and walked.

It was on that first march, through woods wet with spiderwebs and mosses, that it took me to think that the one we had left shackled in Paradise had somehow come to walk behind us, that she was shuffling along just off past our eyes, that, just as we were to her, she was bound to us by unbreakable threads. I knew then that my trick to help her free had not worked, that she had sunk down in that shed after we left her there then risen to follow after us. But by daybreak, with Cleome smiling her smile in the gloaming, the shuffling behind us stopped and I knew it was just walking my face through too many spiderwebs in the dark that had turned my mind to ghosts.

I could not speak for some time after we left Paradise, just lay in the back of the cart like that dead thing and tried to remember what had always once seemed to me to be so beautiful about the old blue sky and its clouds. As a girl I had lain in the grasses of Paradise with daisies in my hair and looked up at the clouds. I had shut my eyes with those daisies in my hair and wished that my sister and me could live up amongst them. Lying in the back of the cart I could hear the breeze blowing across those grasses I lay in as a girl. With my eyes shut I could feel the daisies sweet and soft in my hair. I could not make the blue sky and the clouds above me look like anything except the witness to what should never have been allowed to happen. The witness that had just looked on and on and on.

When we got close to Louisville, and Prosper had stopped the horses under a tree to rest them, I told him that now he had been to the place where his mother and his aunt had faced their travails. He had been to a place of hurt and murder, to a place where we had suffered and handed out suffering, to a place I had never thought to see again.

"Who is Ginestra Lancaster?" Prosper asked.

There is a scar on my face that leads from my left temple to the bottom of my left cheek. It was not allowed to heal properly and even all these years later it looks raw. When he was a small boy, and one or the other of us was sad and looking for comfort, Prosper took the habit of tracing that scar, gently, with his finger, like it was the trail he needed to follow to get us where we needed to go. Sitting in that cart, under that tree, I took up his big hand and ran his long finger down that scar and said, "Ginestra Lancaster is the one who gave me that."

Prosper sat silent with his finger on my cheek. There were frogs at work in some nearby pond and big black dragonflies haunted the trees. Prosper looked off into the green and blue and ran his finger up past my eye then back down again.

"And why are we looking for Ginestra Lancaster now?" he asked.

"Because I have something to return to her," I said.

"Hate returns hate, Aunt Z," said Prosper.

"Yes," I said.

I took his hand and held my face against it for a long time.

It had been given to me to lead us the thirty miles to the crossing place. I was young and had my good young eyes, and there was no longer any shuffling along behind us, but on our second night I let us get lost. Cleome had asked to sit for a moment, so I had let her sit and both of us fell asleep the second we touched ground. When we woke I did not know how long we had slept, and fearing the light that might come at any minute hurried us off on our way. We had each of us had a dream while we slept, and I could see the trouble of it in Cleome's eyes and feel the trouble of it in myself, and in this trouble and hurry I took us off on the wrong way.

How long we wandered as I tried to retrieve our lost path I don't know. Clouds hung low and the wood was thick. Once I fell into a gully and tore my dress on a thorn slick. Cleome caught her hair on an oak branch. An owl came swooping by. Near sunrise it took me to run. I don't know why it came upon me that we must. We ran and crossed a road and had just gotten over it safely to the other side when a cart came along. Cleome breathed loud beside me and had been struck by a cough. I told her to cover her mouth and lie low, and she smiled her little smile at me and did her best. I don't know why I had felt we needed to run, what had frightened me. There were two white men sitting at the front of the cart, one of them looking sharp and holding a rifle. In the back of the cart sat another man with a rifle and beside him a white man wrapped in chains. Just as they were passing Cleome coughed loud, and all four of them turned their heads. It was only one of them who found my eyes in the grasses, the one dressed in chains. I did not move and I did not blink, and the man saw me and I saw him. It was Bennett Marsden, friend to our dead owner. His lips curled a little and his eyebrow went up, then he looked away and the cart rolled on.

I took us farther into the wood away from the road, and we waited the long day under an ash tree, Cleome coughing and smiling and speaking about her rocks. She said she was glad we had run through the dark woods, that the rocks had fallen away from her faster as we had. With the light I could figure where we were and where we needed to be and felt calmed by this knowledge. We had long had the habit of telling little stories to each other, sometimes about our lost brother Alcofibras, and the strange chance of seeing Bennett Marsden, who had known us all in the old days before Paradise, all wrapped up in chains made me think of him. So I told the story of how Alcofibras had one day, when he had been let to wander a little, come upon a fish that had tried to swallow a snake and was now floating dead with it still caught in its jaws. Alcofibras had gone down into the pond and pulled the snake out of the fish's mouth, and the snake had woken and looked Alcofibras in the eye then had slithered off. "That's us, slithering off now," I told Cleome.

"Taken out of the fish's mouth," she said.

"Still alive."

"Still alive, yes, but slithering off where? That's what I'm trying to figure. And to what?"

We returned the cart and horses to their owner in Louisville then took the train to Indianapolis. Eunice Fairbanks's daughter lives there with her husband in a nice little home and when we called at her door she invited us to stay with her. I was as pleased as Prosper was to accept the invitation. Lilly Fairbanks had been a student at the same time as Prosper in the classroom where I worked as a teacher's assistant in Chicago for thirty years. She was as sweet and sharp as ever, and before we knew it we had our feet up and lemonade in our hands.

"Well now, Miss Zinnia, what brings you and Prosper to Indianapolis?" she said, taking a seat near us.

"I hardly know," I said.

That evening before we slept, I told Prosper that I was worn out and would need to recuperate for a few days before continuing on our way. He said he understood and wondered what I thought about him taking a trip ahead up into Clinton County for us. He wouldn't do any talking beyond asking directions, beyond finding our path, if it could be found. That way, when I was ready, we could head straight for Mr. Lucious Wilson's door. It was something he could do and do easily for me, he said. He is a very good boy, is my Prosper. He is my dearest heart on this earth. There isn't anyone else I would have let share my errand, and I told him so.

"What is your errand, Aunt Zinnia?"

I shrugged, and he shrugged and smiled, and I promised I would tell him—as I now am telling you, you and the one other who I now think needs to read this—soon enough.

While he was gone the next whole day and a half, I lay on the bed Lilly Fairbanks had let me have the use of and looked the past in its eye. It peered in at me through the window and down at me from the ceiling, and more than once it crawled right up and sat down hard on my chest. They say once you've had the shackle on you it never comes off. I know one of our flock on the South Side can't look at his legs without seeing chains. I could feel it as I lay there—around my neck, around my ankle, around my arm. There is being whipped and then there is being whipped when you are tied to an oak tree in the noonday sun. Who can you tell that to? Who has the ears to hear it? I save it for my prayers. There are a good number of us now in the County Home. Our church takes food to them each month.

I never cry, but I cried a little as I lay on Lilly Fairbanks's clean sheets with the past sitting on my chest, its black eyes peering down at me. I suppose I thought I would like to just leave it behind and go home to my own room in Prosper's house in Chicago. Maybe Ginestra Lancaster was dead now. Maybe it was too late. I could return to my church and Prosper could go back to his work and the past could go back to mostly ignoring me. But there I was and there it was. I neither blinked nor turned away from it. Where could I have looked?

As we sat waiting for nightfall, Cleome calmed herself down out of a coughing fit then said it was her turn to tell me a story. She said she could not remember if Alcofibras or some other had first told it to her. Or, in truth, if anyone had told it to her at all. It was long ago, at the beginning of everything, and in those early days all the people were just skulls. They had no arms, no legs, no bodies, no skin, no eyes. They were skulls with little candle flames burning inside of them, and to get around they had to hop. They were always angry, these skulls, and they were jealous of the animals that walked the earth with their paws and green eyes and long teeth and handsome fur. Whenever they could they would kill an animal and steal its fur and take its eyes and walk through the world clothed in something besides bone and with something to see with that wasn't candle flame.

One day the lord of fire, who ruled over that world, went out for a walk and saw a group of these skulls stalk and kill and skin a beautiful lion. He watched them fight over the skin and the eyes and the legs and the claws. They fought so hard that everything was torn to bits and all that was left was a bloody mess. He was saddened by this sight and walked on. A little farther along he saw a group of skulls stalk and kill and skin a beautiful deer. He watched them fight over the skin and the eyes and the legs and the hooves. He was saddened by this sight and shook his head and walked on. All of that day and all of that night he watched skulls stalk and kill and destroy, and what they didn't destroy they paraded around in. Sometime during the middle of that night, he came upon a group of the skulls huddled quietly together in a pile, their little candle flames gently lighting the night. He was so struck by the difference between these skulls and the ones he had seen before that he asked them why they, too, weren't fighting over a carcass, why they were sitting so quietly with their candles burning so bright.

"Shhh," they said to him, "There's an elephant coming. We mean to have its tusks."

The lord of fire was so disgusted by all these skulls that he sent out a cold wind to blow out their candles. When all the candles of the world had been blown out, he gathered up the skulls and built fine bodies around them and wrapped skin around the bodies and gave them all eyes and mouths and ears. "You are the people I meant," he said, considering them as they rose and began to walk about. Then he went back to his palace to sleep. While he slept the people put on clothes and built themselves houses and ploughed the fields and harvested their grains. It was while they were working, and while the lord of fire was sleeping, dreaming his dreams of fire, that in some of their skulls, some of the candle flames came flickering back.

It took Cleome quite some time to tell me this story, and when she had finished her eyes were closed and she was so quiet I thought she must have dozed. It was closing in on dusk, and I knew we both needed the rest, so I wrapped my arms tight around her and closed my eyes too. It wasn't more than a few seconds later though that she said, "I saw those candle flames burning in his eyes. That's how he could see his way to us in the dark. You think there are some can see in the dark up there in the North too? Some to come heavy boot down the hallway toward you?"

After Prosper had returned and I had had my rest, we hired another wagon and rode up from Indianapolis to Clinton County so that I could return to Ginny Lancaster what all those years before she had given me. Lilly Fairbanks and her husband told us, as they had told Prosper some days before, that we should not go up to Clinton County, where they were as likely to put a rope to colored people as help them on their errands, no matter how light-skinned they might be, but I said that I must go, and Prosper said that if I was going he was going, and that at any rate he'd already been up there and had only been treated to a few ill-colored words. After we had ridden away I asked him if it was true that he hadn't been too badly treated, and he said it was true, although that might have been because he was on a good horse and had tried to look like he was on somebody else's business, which he was. He said he knew that some of them had seen what he was, there were always some, but no one had tried to stop him, no one had interfered.

It took us until the middle of the afternoon to reach the fine house of Lucious Wilson, deep in the green cornfields of Clinton County, Indiana, and this time, when we had reached our destination, I found I did not need to stay in the cart, but walked straight up to the front door and knocked. My knock was answered by a small white woman in her middle years, who smiled up at me. I had been prepared for her to shut the door in my face or to tell me that the servants' entrance was around the side or to treat me or Prosper poorly in some other way, but she did not. In fact, she turned her smile over to Prosper, who had stayed with the wagon. She even gave him a wave.

"I am here to speak to Mr. Lucious Wilson," I said. "I do beg your and his pardon for any trouble."

"No trouble at all," she said. "Will you come in?"

It was as fine a home on the inside as it had looked on the outside. The floors had been stained and swept clean and there were no cobwebs in the corners. Books lined the walls, and there was a long curl to the banister that led up the stairs. The woman offered me a comfortable chair in the parlor, but I stood in the entrance hall with my travel hat in my hand. While I waited, I looked at a piece of stitch-work made by someone who had known her business. The stitchwork had a silver frame and a border of flowers. In the middle of it, curled around a sleeping child, was the Lord's Prayer.

"You will sit with me as we speak," said Mr. Lucious Wilson when he came. There wasn't any question to it, so I followed him into the parlor and sat. His daughter, for that was who the woman was, brought us cool blackberry tea, then went out the front door and carried a glass of it to Prosper and told him to take his cart over near the shed where the horses could stand out of the sun.

Lucious Wilson was every bit as old as I was and had some trouble with his breath. When he had caught it, he said, "I saw that fellow the other day and thought he was white, now I can see that he is not."

"My nephew."

"I expect I would have to see you stand together."

"There is a resemblance. Some have said he takes a good deal after me."

"You look like you've been on the road a spell."

"Yes sir, I have."

"And where have you come from?"

"Chicago."

"Went there once. Long ago. Before the big buildings. What I wanted to ask you was where you *come* from."

"Below the river," I said. It was the simplest way to say it.

"Kentucky," he said.

I nodded. We sat quietly. The house had many a modest creak. We breathed and listened to them. Or I listened to them. After a time, he spoke.

"You were down there with our Sue, weren't you?"

"Sue, sir?"

"Ginny. Ginestra Lancaster. Down *there* with her."

Lucious Wilson shuddered just the tiniest bit as he said this. I did not shudder, not even that small amount, nor did I answer, but thought of the stitchwork in the entrance hall. I had the Lord's Prayer on my own wall in Prosper's house in Bronzeville. We said the Lord's Prayer every Sunday at my church. The Lord's Prayer, I had always found, could never be used up. All I ever had to do was lay my eyes or mind on it to feel refreshed. With the Lord's Prayer, I was stronger than it all.

"Isn't that what this is? Isn't that who you and that nephew of yours looks like a white boy are?" he said.

There wasn't anything mean in his voice, only a harshness because of the breath that was leaving him, which was the same breath that was leaving me, that is leaving all of us on this earth.

"A place in Charlotte County. By a stream. The owner, Linus Lancaster, was a pig farmer. There were several of us to start. Then just a few. We called it Paradise," I said.

"Paradise?"

"A greensward out of the old days. I have something to return to her, something she gave me down there. I got my use out of it and have never touched it since. There's more on the coil. I should have left the whole and not just part of it with her in the long ago."

He squinted his eyes, raised a long white eyebrow. I reached into my bag and pulled it out, held it up.

He cleared his throat, took a breath, nodded.

"You know that is her needlework you have been looking at over on the wall yonder," he said.

"Miss Ginny's?"

"Sue's. She hasn't been called Ginestra Lancaster in fifty years."

"Sue's," I said.

"Would you say it with me?"

"Yes sir."

So we bowed our heads and said the Lord's great prayer together, then he stood and told me where she lived.

Cleome's time came as we were crossing a ditch next to a barley field gone badly to seed. It flung her down onto the hard dirt and would not let her rise. They had told me there would be a woman who could help us at the crossing place, but it was still some miles away and I did not dare leave.

She smiled, did my younger sister Cleome, in between her screams. She said the rocks were still falling out of her pockets, that she felt lighter each minute, that everything now was soft and sweet. She pushed and she pushed. "Pray with me," she said near the end. I put my face against hers and I did. "Sing to me," she said. I gathered her into my arms and sang. There was a song she wanted from her girlhood. A song from our mother. "Yes," she said as I sang it. She was as brave in that ditch as anything that ever walked through this world.

I left the child in the pool of blood it had made and went on to the crossing place. When I got there, they said they thought it was two of us. I said it was three, maybe more, maybe all of Kentucky. When I said this, I turned on my heel and ran all the way back to that ditch. The child lay untouched. I cut the cord, wrapped him up, then covered my sister with rocks. Then I realized what I had done and pulled every one of those rocks off of her and hid her in some brush. I sat there beside that brush a long time until the baby in my arms began to cry. At the crossing place they looked us up and down for a long time. "Where is the mother?" they asked me.

"I made us run," I said. "I got us lost."

The little house Lucious Wilson had given to Ginny Lancaster sat one mile away from his big one at the end of a stand of shagbark hickory and giant white oak. There was a fine field behind it and a few brave flowers poking up out of a black bed on the front lawn. This time I had Prosper get out of the wagon with me and come to the front door. I stood there looking at its fresh yellow paint for a long time without knocking then took the spool with its few last lengths of purple thread out of my bag and set it down on the porch. It didn't look like much. Any kind of a wind would have blown it out into the field.

"All right," I said.

"All right, Aunt Zinnia," said Prosper.

We were almost to the cart when the door behind us opened

I could not see her at first, there in the gloom.

All those years, all those miles.

"Please," she said. "Come back. Come in."

A woman gave me a blanket for the child, said he looked strong, asked me if I planned to keep him.

"Keep him?" I said. "He is my nephew. He is my own."

They put oar to water at dusktime, took us out across the darkening waters. The child cried but a little as we went toward the lights on the far bank. I named him when we were halfway home.

THE STONECUTTER'S TALE

(BY THE RIVER, BY THE WORLD)
1930

but for every trifle are they set upon me

I HAVE TWO VOICES. One I use when I am at home and one I use when I am anywhere else. I sat down in the booth and used the second one. The waitress brought me a cup of coffee. When she set it down in front of me, I used the voice again and asked for a slice of pie.

"You want whipped cream with that, hon?" she asked me.

I shook my head.

She brought me a glass of ice water with the pie. There was a fan turning noisily on the ceiling. She had sweated the armpits out of her uniform. She looked tired. Too worn out for the job. Her uniform too snug.

"Come far?" she asked me.

"Illinois," I said.

"All that way?"

I nodded.

"First time?"

"No," I said. "I've been down here before. Came on a visit with my aunt. It has been awhile though."

I had spent the morning on the Ohio in a rented boat I had barely been able to steer. Twice I had run aground on sandbars. I am too old to pole heavy boats off sandbars, but I had done it each time. Aunt Z told me, before she died, that if I ever went looking, I should keep an eye out for a lone, brown bluff on the far side of the water. I had seen it long after I had lost hope.

"There's a house down by the river. A big white house with a green roof. How do I get there?" I asked the waitress when she came over with the coffeepot.

"Why do you want to go *there*?" the waitress said.

"It's where I'm bound," I said.

She looked at me, raised her eyebrow. I counted three fat droplets of sweat hanging from its curling tines. One of them dropped as I watched. She wiped the others away. I knew she couldn't tell, hadn't seen it yet, but it was in the room with us now, was ambling along the line of booths toward us, would come and sit down beside me, would curl my straight hair and darken my light skin. When I was young I had my smile and my fresh, unlined young face to send it away when I had to, but those days are long gone. Still, I had my traveling voice, my Main Street voice.

"This pie is delicious," I said.

"I baked it myself," she said.

"I might have guessed. I might just have guessed."

I ate my pie, drank my coffee, got my directions. I was waving good-bye when I stepped out the front door and only narrowly avoided colliding with a man and a woman dressed in old horse blankets and wearing feathers in their

hair. They nodded at me and I nodded back, then I
watched them cross the street and disappear into a stand of
trees beyond a filling station just like they had never been.

The house sat on a rise above the river. I left my tools in
the car and walked down a narrow lane from the road. The
front door opened before I had crossed the scraggly lawn.
A woman in her later years stood before me. She had on a
clean blue dress. She looked up at me through heavy spec-
tacles.

"Can I do for you?" she said.

"I am a reporter for the *Chicago Sun,* and I am writing
an article on places where slaves were given help. I understand this was one."

I had spent time memorizing this speech during the
drive down. I have never been a reporter for the *Chicago Sun*
or for any other paper, but I did once, briefly, before I took
up my trade, think of becoming one.

"I don't know anything about that," she said.

"I'm very sorry to hear it."

"We don't keep with coloreds here."

"I understand."

"Who told you about this place? They been talking in
town?"

I shook my head. The house was in bad shape but didn't
look old enough to have been standing for better than sev-
enty years. One or two of the outbuildings, possibly.

"Is there someone else I might speak to? Someone who
might direct me?"

"I'm it," she said. "Last one standing."

"I know how that feels."

"Do you?"

"Yes, I do."

"Well, I'm sorry I couldn't be any help to you."

"And I'm sorry for having troubled your afternoon."

"You have other places to visit for your newspaper article?"

"Just this one."

I had turned and started across the lawn. I had begun to walk back to my car, to return from nothing to nothing, the air, the road, the long drive back, when she spoke.

"My parents were Christian people," she said.

I stopped.

"They said the good Lord saw no color when he looked down at us."

I had put my hat back on. I took it off again.

"No color at all."

I nodded. She looked carefully at me.

"You don't look anything like a reporter," she said.

I nodded again.

She stood without moving for a long time, then she clicked her tongue and gave me a small, careful smile.

We crossed what had once possibly been a sorghum field, then followed a path down a gulley, through a notch between two hills and into a pretty stand of oak, willow, and birch. I took my hat off and held it against my chest when she pointed. Two or three dozen moss-dripping markers sat surrounded by the remnants of an iron fence. The markers were cross-shaped. Made of pink granite most of them.

"Some didn't make it across the river. My parents buried every last one."

I nodded. I'd heard about that.

"Who you looking for?" she said.

"Her name was Cleome."

"No Cleomes here," she said.

I was walking the markers, the woman stepping quietly behind me.

"I know every name. If they had one. Josiah, Eunice, Claremont, Osa, Letty, Brister, Dorcas, Jupiter, Pompey, Fanny, Turquoise, Lince."

I turned. The woman had stopped. Was looking up at me.

"What's your given name?"

I told her.

"We've met before."

I shook my head, smiled. She did not.

"I used to ride the boat when they made the crossing. My daddy said we were doing Christian work. Told me to come along. You got your name on that boat. Your aunt called it out. We all heard it."

"Yes ma'am," I said.

"They burned my parents out during the war. Said they were helping other people's property escape. They hung my daddy from a tree."

"Yes ma'am."

"My mother rebuilt. She lived to be a hundred."

I nodded.

"That's your mother there."

I followed her arm to a marker at the back of the ceme-
tery. She let me walk over alone. There was moss in the
grooves but the inscription could still be read.

Mother of Prosper
1861

"My Daddy went out and found her where she passed.
Brought her here on the mule wagon. She got her Christian
rights as best as they could be given."

It took me a long time to be able to speak. I used my
first voice when I did.

"Then I'm obliged to your father."

"No," she said. "No, you aren't."

"Then to you."

"Not to me either."

She started to walk back the way they had come, called
over her shoulder as she was walking: "There's room for
her name on there. I know a stonecutter in town wouldn't
ask any questions."

But I had already seen where I would make my first
cut.

LUCIOUS

(AGONISTES)
1912

Here; swear then how thou escapedst

THERE IS A STORY goes with my name too. I was to have been called Joseph after the grand old man and be done with it. I was to have been Joseph Aloysius Wilson and that's that. I was fresh born and on the earth and had my name. Then my father had his vision. Out in the field in the middle of the bright sunshine with his eyes still open but for the blinks. In it just born as I was, he carried me on his back all the way to North Carolina where I had started my dark swim. My mother stayed behind in Indiana, and my father carried me away from barley and corn and back into cotton and tobacco. He followed the route they had taken in riding away from it all, and he knew the road every inch and mile. I did not cry on his back, just rode along like a soft doll, and when he was again on the farm they had left behind there was no one but a colored woman waiting there. All the others had gone like my parents had, and it was just an old colored woman he had never laid eyes on before. She was dressed in drab except for a crimson scarf. In her hands she held a package tied with string. My father reached for the package, but she shook her head, so he reached behind him and hefted me around and she put it in my hands. When she had completed this chore, she touched my forehead and nodded at my father and was gone.

"Well, open it," my father told me, even though I had just been born. I opened it and fetched out a slip of paper had on it a single word.

"Lucious," my father told my mother when he was awake to the world again and had got back to what wasn't yet quite a house.

"He will be called Joseph as we planned. As he already is," said my mother.

"Lucious is his name," my father said.

"You just fell asleep and had a dream."

"I wasn't asleep."

"His name is Joseph."

"Lucious is what he will be called."

My father said it one more time, and then he took up his musket and fired it out the window. And that was that, and when in after years I complained about my name no one knew how to say or spell, they would both of them tell me about my father's vision. Didn't stop me from hating it though. The way a child can hate a thing. Hate it to crying, to kicking, to gnashing of tumbledown milk teeth. You will understand why when one Sunday we passed a farm where a colored woman, first I had ever seen, was bent over in an oat field, I wrote my hated name down on a piece of paper and wrapped it up in a package and tied it with string. I waited until my parents weren't likely to look for me and walked four miles back to that farm and handed it to the colored woman, who took it from me without a word.

"My name is Joseph. I don't want your name," I told her. She had green eyes and fine, long eyebrows and wore feathers and strips of string in her hair and was the strangest and handsomest woman I had ever seen.

"I gave it back," I told my father that evening at supper.

"Gave back what?" my father said.

"My name."

"To that red Indian girl?"

"Was she an Indian?"

That is the first part of the story of my name, and I have told it twice in my life to listeners hadn't heard it before. The first time was during the war, when I was sick in love and there was a hurt soldier resting up in the little house I still have here on my property. He had been home to see his parents and was returning to the fight and had had a wound go bad on him. I was sick in love, and the one I was sick in love with was tending his wound and looking soft at him who was curly-haired and green-eyed and not at me who was just an already-old man owned some beasts and land, and when I went down there it was to try and see what it was that soldier had that I didn't. Took about ten seconds to see that he had everything. Everything I was missing. Going back down to war. Probably to get killed. Thunder and glory. Sulfur and bayonet. Clear road to the beyond.

He was young and sick and asked me to hold his hand, grip it tight. I held his hand and told him the story of my name. He had his fever and didn't hear it. I know because when the fever broke a week later, I asked him if he remembered what my name was supposed to have been, should have been, and when I smiled and asked this, he looked at me strange. So I bade him farewell and sent him down to rejoin his regiment on one of my good mules. As he rode off, the one I was sick in love with and who wasn't sick or any other ways in love with me whispered out at him, "Good-bye, Joseph."

She was the other I told the story to. I told it to her not a season ago. In that same little house, which for the fifty years after that soldier's leaving I saw to it was her house. Of course it is now no longer her house because she is also gone. Vanished up the chimney with its ash.

"I have always liked that name of yours," she said. She was old and stout and rattled like a boiler, but she said it and dug a tear out of my eye.

"Call me Joseph," I said. "Call me Joseph and I will call you Ginny, and we will be called by our true names."

"My name is Sue. Add on Scary if you want."

"I never called you Scary."

"And your name is Lucious."

"Why wouldn't you have me?"

She was wearing a ring woven out of purple thread on one of her fingers. She did not give an answer. Had already given it. Lifetime ago. She pointed with that finger to a large, thick envelope with a Chicago send-back address printed on it in neat handwriting that was foreign to me. Then she pointed at a thicker stack of papers sitting near it, which she had covered in her own hand.

"There's true stories there if you care to read them," she said. "Mine and hers both. You know who it is I mean."

Then she asked me if after she was gone I would send her stack, along with a word or two of my own if I wanted, to the Chicago address the thick envelope had sailed down to her from.

"Don't you die on me, Sue," I said.

"Swear to me you will send it," she said.

"I swear it," I said.

"Lucious. Lucious Wilson," she said.

There is snow come up as I have told the story of my name. Snow and small smacks of hail on the roof of this little house.

I went then I came back then I went then I came back again. In going I came and in coming I went. In that way I didn't need to see an inch of my road and might as well have took out my own eyes. But here they still are—candy jellies, each afloat, each in its own glass jar.

COLOPHON

Kind One was designed at Coffee House Press,
in the historic Grain Belt Brewery's Bottling House
near downtown Minneapolis.
The text is set in Goudy Village.

MISSION

The mission of Coffee House Press is to publish exciting, vital, and enduring authors of our time; to delight and inspire readers; to contribute to the cultural life of our community; and to enrich our literary heritage. By building on the best traditions of publishing and the book arts, we produce books that celebrate imagination, innovation in the craft of writing, and the many authentic voices of the American experience.

VISION

LITERATURE. We will promote literature as a vital art form, helping to redefine its role in contemporary life. We will publish authors whose groundbreaking work helps shape the direction of 21st-century literature.

WRITERS. We will foster the careers of our writers by making long-term commitments to their work, allowing them to take risks in form and content.

READERS. Readers of books we publish will experience new perspectives and an expanding intellectual landscape.

PUBLISHING. We will be leaders in developing a sustainable 21st-century model of independent literary publishing, pushing the boundaries of content, form, editing, audience development, and book technologies.

VALUES

Innovation and excellence in all activities

Diversity of people, ideas, and products

Advancing literary knowledge

Community through embracing many cultures

Ethical and highly professional management
and governance practices

Join us in our mission at coffeehousepress.org

FUNDERS

Coffee House Press is an independent, nonprofit literary publisher. Our books are made possible through the generous support of grants and gifts from many foundations, corporate giving programs, state and federal support, and through donations from individuals who believe in the transformational power of literature. Coffee House Press receives major operating support from the Bush Foundation, the Jerome Foundation, the McKnight Foundation, the National Endowment for the Arts—a federal agency, from Target, and in part, from the Minnesota State Arts Board through the arts and cultural heritage fund as appropriated by the Minnesota State Legislature with money from the Legacy Amendment vote of the people of Minnesota on November 4, 2008. Coffee House also receives support from: several anonymous donors; Suzanne Allen; Elmer L. and Eleanor J. Andersen Foundation; Around Town Agency; Patricia Beithon; Bill Berkson; the E. Thomas Binger and Rebecca Rand Fund of the Minneapolis Foundation; the Patrick and Aimee Butler Family Foundation; Ruth Dayton; Dorsey & Whitney, LLP; Mary Ebert and Paul Stembler; Chris Fischbach and Katie Dublinski; Fredrikson & Byron, P.A.; Sally French; Anselm Hollo and Jane Dalrymple-Hollo; Jeffrey Hom; Carl and Heidi Horsch; Alex and Ada Katz; Stephen and Isabel Keating; the Kenneth Koch Literary Estate; Kathy and Dean Koutsky; the Lenfestey Family Foundation; Carol and Aaron Mack; Mary McDermid; Sjur Midness and Briar Andresen; the Rehael Fund of the Minneapolis Foundation; Schwegman, Lundberg & Woessner, P.A.; Kiki Smith; Jeffrey Sugerman; Patricia Tilton; the Archie D. & Bertha H. Walker Foundation; Stu Wilson and Mel Barker; the Woessner Freeman Family Foundation; Margaret and Angus Wurtele; and many other generous individual donors.

To you and our many readers across the country, we send our thanks for your continuing support.

OTHER BOOKS BY LAIRD HUNT

Ray of the Star
978-1-56689-232-2

In a dreamlike European city, along a boulevard teeming with living statues, a man is running from his past, a woman is consumed by grief, shoes lead their wearers astray, and all must learn what it means to travel along the ray of the star.

The Impossibly
978-1-56689-281-0

When the anonymous narrator botches an assignment from the clandestine organization that employs him, everyone in his life becomes a participant in his punishment. His final assignment: to seek and identify his own assassin.

The Exquisite
978-1-56689-187-5

Henry, left destitute by circumstance and obsession, is plucked from vagrancy by a shadowy outfit that stages the murders of anxiety-ridden clients seeking to experience—and live through—their own carefully executed assassinations.

Indiana, Indiana
978-1-56689-144-8

As a young man, Noah fell deeply in love with Opal, a young woman with a penchant for flames. On a dark winter night, he will sift through his memories, trying to make sense of a lifetime of psychic visions and his family's tumultuous history.